## ACCLAIM FOR MUSTANG TO PADUCAH

**"Fresh. Gonzo. Ripe for adaptation."**
James Chatterton - Story Analyst at HBO

**"Hip. Smartly-written. An epic journey of the soul."**
Jess Montgomery - Award-winning author and journalist

**"An engaging, evocative book filled with great period detail."**
Ralph Keyes - Author of *The Post-Truth Era*

**"Fast-paced. Witty. Raul Ramos y Sanchez is a master storyteller."**
John Kachuba - Author of *Shapeshifters: A History*

**"What a pleasure, this endlessly inventive book."**
John Thorndike - Author of *The World Against Her Skin*

**"Madcap. Entertaining. Could easily become a TV series."**
Marco Frazier - Global Media Executive

## RECOGNITION FOR AUTHOR RAUL RAMOS Y SANCHEZ

Books Into Movies Award Winner, presented by Edward James Olmos

Violet Crown Fiction Award Finalist, Writers League of Texas

Best Novel, International Latino Book Awards

Selected for Los Angeles Magazine's "The Reading List"

LATINA Magazine "Hot Summer Reads" Author

USA Today Summer Reads Author

Ohioana Book Festival Featured Author

Beck and Branch Publishers
New York, NY | beckandbranch.com
ISBN: 978-0-9994457-7-8

# MUSTANG TO PADUCAH

RAUL RAMOS Y SANCHEZ

BECK AND BRANCH PUBLISHERS

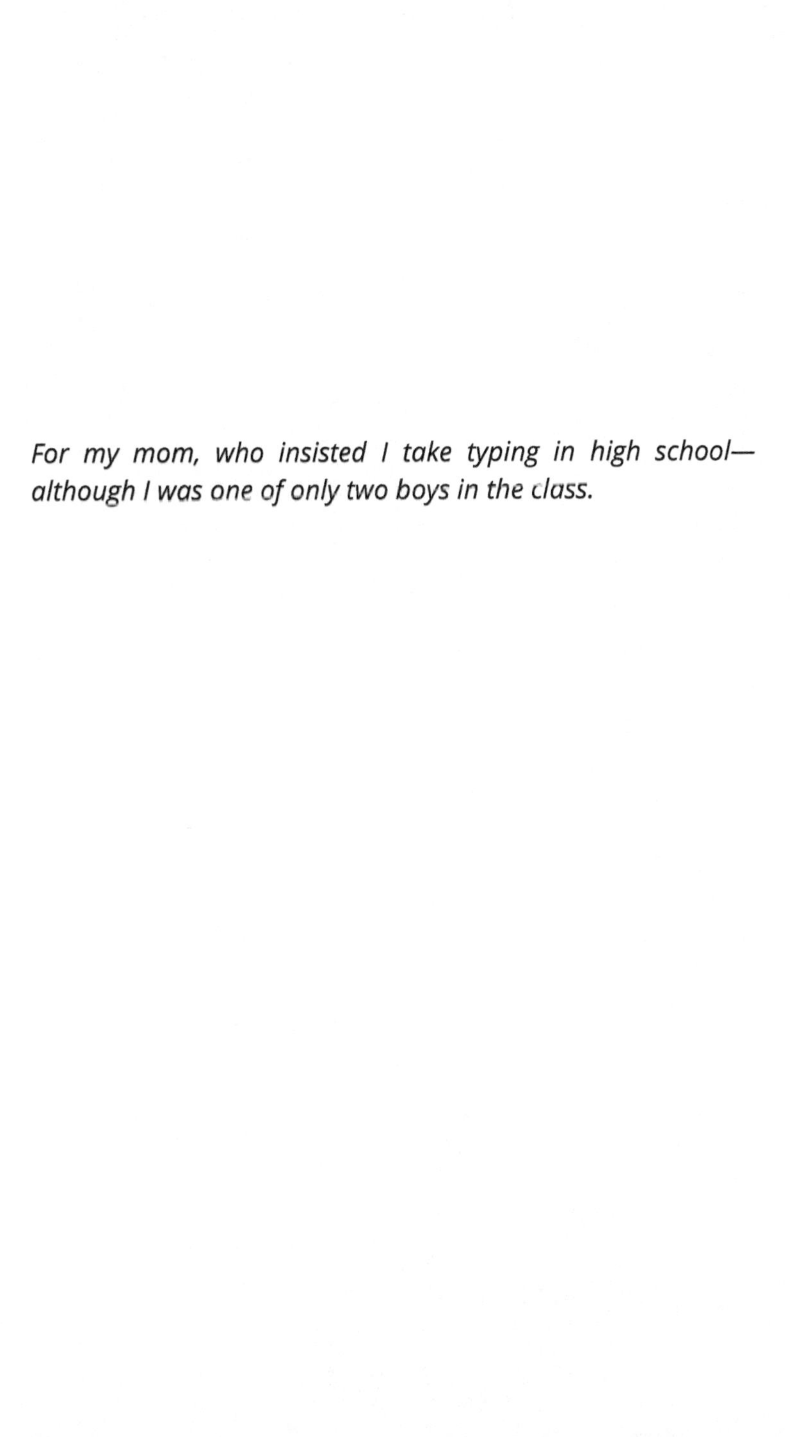

*For my mom, who insisted I take typing in high school—although I was one of only two boys in the class.*

**UNTIL YESTERDAY,** I'd never been north of West Palm Beach. And once this shit was over, man, I'd never leave Miami again.

Peanut and I had passed the last vestiges of civilization after we stopped for gas and munchies in Nashville. Now we were in the boonies of Kentucky on a two-lane through the woods with more ups and downs than getting laid on a waterbed.

I'm a city boy and driving in the middle of nowhere freaks me out – even in broad daylight.

Besides, I had a lot on my mind.

I was totally zoned on avoiding the potholes. The last few miles of road could have been the training site for a moon landing. And I sure as hell didn't want to ding this sweet '69 aqua blue Mustang that still had that sexy new car smell.

Meantime, Peanut was in the seat beside me rattling off directions while Hendrix blared from the 8-track. Okay, there was another thing messing with my head. I was still a little buzzed from the joint we'd fired up about thirty miles back.

Next thing I know, Peanut lets go with a spit-flying scream. "I said STOP, man! We missed our turn!"

I hit the brakes hard, slamming Peanut into the dashboard.

"Goddamit, Cruiser!" Peanut rubbed the goose egg rising on his forehead. "Your hearing needs some glasses, man."

I turned off the 8-track. "Sorry. I kinda spaced out," I said, glad as hell the dash was padded. "Are you okay?"

"I'll be fine," he huffed, too cocky to show any pain. Being half baked helped.

"Where was I supposed to turn?"

Peanut pointed through the rear window to a narrow gravel path that disappeared into the trees. "Back there."

"Are you sure?"

"Yeah, goddamit. Look." Peanut held out the hand drawn map that had gotten us this far. "It says 'next right after the Clarks River bridge.' This is it, man."

"How could anybody live there? That's not even a street."

"Cruiser, I've got family in Georgia who live down a lane just like that. We're not in Miami anymore, man."

"No shit, Sherlock," I said, turning the Mustang around. "We're in Tobacco goddam Road."

The gravel crunching under the tires drowned out the Mustang's engine as we started down a path through the woods just wide enough for a car. The trees around us were mostly bare.

Holding a half-cold can of Pepsi to the bump on his

forehead, Peanut said, "Don't get too close to the branches, Cruiser. You're gonna scratch the paint."

"Hey, man! If Vardon really lives back here, he should be used to losing some paint," I said. "But if he doesn't, I'm going to let you explain the scratches on his Mustang."

"Screw you, Cruiser. Just be careful."

After driving through the woods for what seemed like forever, I was starting to get freaked. "You see a house yet? 'Cause if we don't get someplace where I can turn around soon, I'll have to back all the way out of here."

"There it is!" Peanut said, pointing to a two-story A-frame cabin peeking through the tree trunks. A pickup, and two cars were parked close to the house.

"Yeah? Well, you better hope that's where Vardon lives," I said, pulling up to the cabin, "and not Gomer Pyle's evil twin who shoots hippies on sight." Our long hair and bell bottoms had earned us some hard looks every time we'd stopped for gas or food in Grand Ole Opry country.

I turned off the engine and buttoned up my jean jacket. March was a lot colder up here than in Miami. When I got out of the car, I took two steps and stopped in my tracks.

An eerie wail was coming from the house – like the music in a sci-fi flick when the evil aliens are about to land. "What's that?" I asked Peanut, my knees a little wobbly.

"I don't know, man. Maybe we should knock and find out," he said, walking toward the door.

"Maybe we should come back later," I said, sliding back into the car.

"Hey! Come here, chickenshit! We drove two days to get here and now you're going to freak out over some strange noise? We promised to bring this car here – and I'm not giving up on that thousand bucks they owe us."

Ashamed but still leery, I got out of the car. "Man, you're going to get us killed one of these days."

"Cruiser, you're such a pussy," Peanut said in disgust, then knocked on the door.

As we waited, my stomach was turning cartwheels. Here we were, two hippies in the middle of the sticks, knocking at a strange house with a scary-movie soundtrack. I was ready for a seven-foot, shotgun-toting bubba to open the door – or maybe brain-eating aliens.

When no one answered, Peanut knocked again. After a moment, he turned the handle and opened the door.

I almost shit.

"What the hell are you doing?" I said, trying to hold him back.

Peanut pushed my hand away. "We've got to find Vardon and get our money, man" he said, walking inside.

I stood frozen in the doorway as all five-foot-seven and 130 pounds of Peanut O'Connor disappeared around a corner inside the dimly lit house.

Since we were kids, that boy had always had more guts than gray matter. I was four inches taller and outweighed him by forty pounds. But I'd always avoided tangling with the little shit.

"Cruiser! Come here!" Peanut yelled over the screeching. There was fear in his voice.

Heart in my throat, I went inside.

In a large room, I saw Peanut standing over four bleeding bodies sprawled on the floor – and found the source of the weird noise. It was the feedback from a Marshall amp.

The dead guys were a band, gunned down while they were practicing. A couple of the Glen Campbell looking dudes on the floor still had guitars strapped on their shoulders. Another one was near a drum set. They'd knocked over microphone stands and amplifiers as they fell, creating the feedback.

Peanut pointed to a blond guy among the bodies. "That one's Vardon. I recognize him from the pictures Donnie showed us," he yelled over the feedback. "What the hell do we do now?"

# 2

## FIVE DAYS EARLIER

**THE MACAQUE** raised his eyebrows, bared his teeth and howled at me.

"Hey, man. Stop being such a badass. I'm doing you a favor," I told the brown monkey squirming in my hands. He wasn't fully grown. Otherwise, he would have shredded my arms – even with the thick leather gloves I was wearing.

"You remind me of Peanut, you scrappy little bastard," I said, taking a banana out of my pocket and putting it in his hands. I looked around the roof to make sure no one was watching. I'd get fired if the bosses caught me.

Then I bent down, placed the monkey on the roof and let him go. "*Buena suerte, amigo,*" I said as the macaque scrambled across the roof clutching the banana and jumped into a mango tree. In another second, he was out of sight.

I smiled walking down the fire escape of Miami Pets International, the exotic animal importer where I worked. A guy from my neighborhood named Skinny who'd worked here for a while had started turning a monkey loose each week. After he left, I kept up the tradition.

Then I realized something.

Getting a paycheck and releasing a monkey on Fridays were the only bright spots of my job.

The thought totally brought me down.

When I'd told my ex-girlfriend Cindy about my weekly thing with the monkeys, she thought I was being cruel.

"Those monkeys aren't meant to live here, Cruiser," Cindy said. "They're going to die."

"I'd rather die free than live in a cage," I told her.

We broke up not long after that.

But that wasn't anything new. A nosy neighbor of mine once said, "Cruiser changes his girlfriends more often than the sheets." It was Peanut's mom, so that's how I heard about it. Anyway, it was hard to argue with Mrs. O.

I never had a problem getting chicks. My problem was staying with them.

Most people I meet these days think that's why they call me Cruiser. But I've had that nickname since I was eleven, right after my father brought us to Miami from Cuba. My name is Nestor Cruz. And in our Spanglish-speaking neighborhood, the kids turned Cruz into Cruiser.

Around the same time, a scrawny kid named Maxwell O'Connor arrived in the neighborhood with his divorced mom from Georgia. He got stuck with Peanut.

The two of us became a pair of mismatched bookends. I leaned on Peanut for his backbone. He leaned on me to find friends. But it would have taken thumbscrews for us to admit this out loud.

That was ten years ago. Ever since, the name Cruiser had come to fit a lot of things about me. Maybe it was fate. Who knows? One thing was sure, though.

Right now, I had a paycheck to burn and a weekend ahead.

## 3

**GRETA TURNED** off the engine on the VW Beetle and sighed. "I might as well save some gas. We're not going anywhere for a while."

"Yeah," I said, looking down the long line of cars along Bayshore Drive, "if this traffic doesn't move soon, the cops are gonna start charging us for parking."

Almost an hour ago, thirteen thousand of us had been on our feet, dancing, toking, snorting and tripping as the Doors ended their concert with an encore of *Light My Fire*. Now, the same crowd was packed into cars and clogging the streets of Coconut Grove. I was bummed and restless. I think everyone else was too.

Maybe all the *perico* going around lately had something to do with it. A lot more people were doing nose candy at concerts and festivals these days. Along with the coke, fights and rip-offs had gone up, too. To a plain-Jane grasshopper like me, *perico* was a vibe killer, man.

From the back seat of the Beetle, I heard Peanut strike a match. "Well, if we're stuck here, we might as well make the best of it," he said, firing up a joint. After taking a hit, Peanut passed me the number.

I took a long toke and handed it to Greta. "The head scene in Miami has become a real drag, man," I said, exhaling a cloud of smoke.

Greta took a dainty little puff and gave the joint back to Peanut. "Oh, c'mon, Cruiser. You know we're really just the flower children's National Guard."

"What's that supposed to mean?" I asked.

"You, me and Peanut have jobs during the week, just like the straights. But on weekends, we get all decked out in our hippie gear and make the scene somewhere. It's not like we live in a commune or anything, honey. That kind of hippie is from Coral Gables. They can afford to be full-time heads. We don't have mommy and daddy paying our tuition so we can drop out of college. We're weekend warriors – like the National Guard."

"That's cold, Greta," I said.

"Me, I love being a part-time hippie. It's almost like being in drag," Greta said, primping in the rear-view mirror, flicking his shoulder-length hair.

"Gross," Peanut said from the back seat. "Now I want a haircut."

Greta laughed. "Peanut, you're always cute when you get all macho like that."

The three of us had known each other since elementary school. When Julio Torres had come out of the closet in the eleventh grade and asked us to call him Greta, Peanut and I freaked out. But after a while, we realized this was still the same funny, generous friend we'd always known.

"Well, you must have been in heaven when Morrison flashed his *pinga*," I said to Greta.

"To tell you the truth, Cruiser, he broke my heart," Greta said, "I didn't see anything – and believe me, I looked. So if Jimmy showed his *pinga*, honey, it sure wasn't much."

I wanted to laugh but couldn't. Greta was right. We were weekend hippies – and not very good ones at that. Sure, we were into the whole peace and love thing. But we'd grown up in Wynwood, a neighborhood where you'd better be ready to bust somebody in the chops if you wanted to keep your lunch money.

A lot of the flower children we hung out with at festivals and concerts came from the suburbs. They were dropping out from a world I'd only seen on *Father Knows Best*.

"Maybe I need to get out of Miami for a while," I said. "Go see the world or something."

"Hey, Uncle Sam will be glad to send you on an all-expense-paid trip to Vietnam, man," Peanut said.

"I'd like to come back in something besides a body bag – which in your case, Peanut, would be a Merita bread wrapper," I said. We could joke about it because, luckily, all three of us had drawn high numbers in the draft lottery.

"What do you expect to find somewhere else, Cruiser?" Greta asked.

I don't know," I said shrugging. "There's got to be something else to do besides getting high and chasing chicks."

"If you're bored with chicks, maybe you should join Greta's team," Peanut said, flashing a smug smile.

"Oooh. Put up your dukes, Cruiser," Greta said, rolling his eyes. "Peanut just stepped into the ring at the wit arena."

I should've shown Peanut some mercy, but I was in a crappy mood. "I'm really flattered by your come on, Peanut," I said. "But you'll go broke buying me enough flowers and candy to let you blow me."

Greta grinned and winked at Peanut. "Stick to fist-fights, honey."

"Screw you, Greta," Peanut said.

Greta fluffed his hair and said, "Dream on, honey."

While Peanut and Greta kept hassling each other, I

drifted back to thinking about my life. I mean, shit. Did I even have a future?

A lot of my Cuban neighbors in Miami had been rich back on the island. Not my family.

In Havana, my dad had been a mechanic who worked with his brother-in-law. They had a two-man trucking company that ran loads all over the island for nickel-and-dime businesses. My uncle owned the truck and my dad kept it running.

In Miami, my dad wound up as a boatyard mechanic working mostly on Class IIs because they had diesels a lot like a truck's. My mother was a seamstress who died when I was born.

Was I going to follow my father and make a living in greasy coveralls? I'd taken some junior college courses. But they turned out to be a drag.

The truth is, I'd always been a closet nerd – quite literally.

I started reading books on my own in junior high, and like all bad habits, it was hard to break. But I'd always kept it on the down low. A bookworm growing up in Wynwood became a bully magnet.

So I stashed my library books, along with two worn copies of Playboy, in a Brillo box on the top shelf of my closet. Peanut was the only one who knew about my secret vice.

"Hey, I think we're finally moving," Peanut said as the car ahead of us started inching forward.

"Are you really serious about getting out of town for a while?" Greta said, starting up the Beetle.

"Maybe. Why are you asking?"

"I know a guy who's looking for someone to drive his

car back to Kentucky."

"Kentucky? Man, they eat hippies for breakfast there, don't they?"

"He's willing to pay a thousand bucks."

Peanut leaned forward and said, "I'll do it."

"Wait a minute, Peanut" I said. "You don't know anything about this guy – and what about your job?"

"Cruiser, I can always get another job in the boat-yards. Why don't we go together, man? We can split the thousand and you'll still come away with more bread than you'd make in a couple of months at work."

"You've been doing too much Toluene, man," I said to Peanut. "It's fried your brain." During breaks at work, Peanut would sneak into a boat cabin and huff on a rag soaked in fiberglass thinner.

"Oh?" Peanut said. "So, you're going to become like some kind of Jane What's-her-name studying monkeys where you work? Grow a pair, Cruiser. That job's a dead-end, man."

I thought about what Peanut said. What the hell was I giving up? A career cleaning monkey shit? There was only one thing I knew for sure. I wanted *something* to change. "Greta, is this guy good for the money?"

"Donny's come down to hit the gay scene in Miami before. He usually stays for a few days, then heads back north. But he always seems to have plenty of coin. Tell you what – I'll introduce you guys to him tomorrow and let you decide."

**PEANUT WHISTLED** softly as the three of us walked toward the white yacht at the end of the marina. "Jesus, that thing is big enough to bowl in."

"Don't even think about taking home any souvenirs, Peanut," I said under my breath as we got near the boat.

"Hi, Donny!" Greta said, waving to a buffed-up guy with platinum hair near the open-air bar in the back of the boat.

"Come aboard," Donny called out smiling.

Greta gave Donny a swishy salute. "Aye, Aye, Skipper!" he said in a painted-toenails voice.

After Greta introduced Peanut and me, I said, "Nice rig you got here, man," trying to sound like I got invited on yachts all the time. "Has she got a CAT or a Cummins?"

"I don't know, Cruiser. I'm just a guest here. You guys want a drink?" he said, fanning his hand over the kind of liquor spread I'd only seen in movies. I didn't know what most of it was, so I asked for a Ballantine. Peanut and Greta did the same.

"Thanks, Donny," I said, eyeing the beer label like they do in commercials.

Drinks in hand, we sat down around a shiny wooden table on the deck.

"I still can't believe you two are from Cuba," Donny said, nodding toward Greta and me. "Hell, you speak English better than I do."

"Most of us who got here before we sprouted pubes lost the accent, honey. I've got an older brother who sounds like Ricky Ricardo," Greta said, giggling as he touched Donny's arm. "They say it's something about the brain."

"I made it just under the wire. I got here at eleven," I added.

Peanut was not in the mood for small talk. "Greta told us you need somebody to drive your car back to Kentucky."

"Actually, it's my cousin Vardon's car. I borrowed it to come down here from Paducah," Donny explained. "But we're leaving tomorrow on a three-week cruise and my cousin needs his car back."

Something Donny said seemed kinda fuzzy. "I guess your cousin wasn't expecting you to be gone this long."

"You're right. I came down here for a few days but… well, I sort of hit it off with someone."

"The guy who owns this boat," I said, getting the picture.

"I didn't think I was that obvious," Donny said, his face flushing.

"You're not," I said. "But partying with Greta, well, the dots aren't that hard to connect. In any case, different strokes for different folks, man."

Peanut nodded. "Yeah, we're cool with you being a homo."

When Donny winced, I said, "Don't mind him. His momma chugged sterno while she was nursing."

Donny looked at us and smiled. "I appreciate that, boys. There's one thing, though… If you decide to take the car back, I hope you won't say anything about who I really am to my cousin Vardon. Most folks back home are not as civilized as you are."

"I understand. No problem, man," I said.

"Okay, suppose we do this, man," Peanut said. "How do we get our thousand bucks?"

"Well, I guess we'll have to trust each other," Donny answered. "The car's worth a lot more than a thousand. So if you decided to steal it, I'd lose. But, thanks to Greta, I'm trusting you boys won't." Donny stopped and took a sip of beer. "On the other hand, you'll have to trust my cousin Vardon will pay you when you return his car. I'll let him know you're coming so he'll have the money ready," he said smiling. "It's a gentleman's agreement, as we say back home."

I was going over the whole thing in my mind when Donny said something else.

"I think it's only fair you boys get some cash for traveling expenses," Donny said, pulling out his wallet and laying five crisp twenties on the table. He then put the car keys on the money and slid it toward us. "By the way, did I tell you Vardon's car is a brand-new Mustang?"

The guy sure knew how to seal a deal.

# 5

**I LOOKED** down at the bodies, heart pounding. Somebody deaf could've heard the goose bumps rising on my arms. "We've got to get out of here," I said to Peanut, backing out of the room.

"Wait," Peanut said, bending over Vardon's body, "Maybe he's still got our money on him."

I grabbed Peanut by the shirt and dragged him out of the house, squirming and kicking.

"Man, are you crazy? Get in the car!" I said shoving him toward the Mustang.

Peanut glared at me and clenched his fists, ready to fight. He wasn't used to me pushing him around.

"Put your *cojones* in neutral for a second and think, Peanut," I said. "Whoever killed those guys could still be around or the heat might show up. Either way, we don't want to be here."

The anger faded from Peanut's eyes – and a healthy dose of fear took its place. "Okay, maybe you're right," he said and jumped into the car.

I floored the Mustang, sending gravel flying.

**STRIDING AWAY** from Jenkins' cabin through the woods, Fish was relieved to be done with this pain-in-the-ass hit.

Each day for nearly two weeks, Fish had parked a rented Ford Fairmont out of sight on a side road nearly a mile from Vardon's A-frame and hoofed it through the woods to stake out the place.

The contract killer had written down the plate numbers of the cars that came and went, then later checked them against the Kentucky DMV to find out who owned them. That's how Fish had discovered Vardon and his band met here to rehearse every Wednesday.

After all that trouble, finishing the work had been easy – a perfect job for an Uzi.

For sure, the hit had been a grind. But the payday would be worth it.

Fish had insisted on 10 large for the job and the bosses in Mobile had agreed. They wanted to send a message that would put the fear of God into small-potato coke dealers like Vardon Jenkins horning in on their turf.

Their plan was simple. Whack Vardon and his band, then plant two kilos of coke in the house. When word of the hit got around, any yahoos pushing blow in Dixie Mafia country would start looking for a safer line of work.

Fish was about halfway back to the rental when the rumble of tires on gravel rose in the distance. A car was approaching Jenkins' cabin.

Breaking into a run, Fish started back toward the A-frame.

When Fish finally reached the edge of the woods, the hired killer spotted a blue Mustang parked alongside the other vehicles at the cabin. Fish had not seen the '69 Mustang at the house before. But from the BMV records, Fish knew it belonged to Vardon. Whoever had arrived in Jenkins' car was inside the cabin.

Fish loaded a fresh clip into the Uzi slung over her shoulder and started toward the house, circling around to the back door. Another body at the scene would only add to the headlines her employers were hoping to make.

Reaching the back door, Fish heard an engine turn over out front, followed by the growl of flying gravel. By the time she reached the front door, the Mustang was rounding a bend in the trees on the narrow lane. Through the car's back window, she saw the shadows of two passengers.

"*Scheisse*," Erna Herring said.

Running back into the house, Fish checked the bedroom closet for the blow she'd planted. She was relieved to find the two keys still there.

All the same, two witnesses had seen her work prematurely. That was unacceptable.

**7**

**THE TREES** along the gravel path were a brown blur outside the windows. By the time we reached the paved road, I was sweating and short of breath.

"Okay, man. Where do we go?" Peanut asked.

"Uh, let's see," I said, my mind racing. "Donny put the name of Vardon's sister on the map he gave us, didn't he?"

"Yeah! You're right!" Peanut said and began digging through the glove box until he found the map. "Here we go. Says her name is Sheri Jean and she works in Paducah at a place called... I can't make out his writing. Can you tell what that says?"

"Never mind. We'll figure it out when we get to Paducah," I said, peeling rubber as I turned right.

There were potholes all over the road but I barreled through them. Peanut bounced like a string puppet every time we hit one. At this point, babying the Mustang was the least of my worries. After all, the owner was dead.

About a mile later, I regretted it.

A loud pop from the back of the car turned into a Ginger Baker drum solo. "Shit! We blew a tire!" I said, pulling to the side of the road.

**GASPING FOR** breath as she reached the rental car, Fish shed her black coveralls, revealing the cardigan and capris she wore underneath. Behind the wheel, she took off a knit cap, tied a scarf around her hair and hit the gas.

Steering with one hand, Fish placed the Uzi on the seat beside her. She'd planned to ditch the summer sausage sized submachine gun in the Ohio River on her way back to Newport. Now, she'd need the piece again.

Tires screeching, Herring turned onto the road toward Paducah. The pair in Jenkins' Mustang would almost certainly head that way.

She'd need to be careful, though. The road was a minefield of potholes. Along with slowing her down, the bumpy road would make it harder to get a kill shot on the driver when she caught up to the Mustang. Fortunately, what the Uzi lacked in accuracy, it made up for in the ability to spray lead.

There was one bright side, Fish reminded herself, rounding yet another corner. This corkscrew of a road was mostly deserted. Almost anyplace she caught up to the Mustang would not have any other witnesses.

Erna's pulse rose and she began to pant. As usual, the chase was exhilarating.

"**KEEP IT** together, Cruiser. We've got a spare," Peanut said, reaching for the door handle.

I grabbed his arm. "Stay inside! We need to hide the car."

Peanut shook his head in disgust. "Cruiser, you're a total wimp," he said as I turned into a tree-lined lane.

Out of sight from the road, we got the jack and spare out of the trunk.

"I'm not sure where to set the jack," Peanut said, checking out the wheel well.

"Two goddam years of vocational classes and you don't know how to change a tire?"

"Sorry, man. Maybe I should have been a junior college philosophy dropout like you."

"Why don't you do something useful, like getting your skinny ass under the car and taking a look?"

As Peanut crawled under the Mustang, I heard a car coming toward us on the road. Not daring to talk, I froze and held my breath. Thankfully, the car didn't stop.

By now, all I could see of Peanut were his legs and feet.

"Cruiser, there's something weird under here." Peanut said from under the car.

"Whatever it is, forget about it. We need to fix this flat and split, man."

"Wait a second," Peanut said. I could hear him tearing at something.

"What the hell are you doing?"

A moment later, Peanut crawled out from under the car, his eyes glowing like a kid on Christmas morning. "Look at this!" he said, holding out a plastic-wrapped bundle of white powder about the size of a loaf of bread. "It looks like pure *perico*, man."

"Hide that, for God's sake," I said looking around, sure that a squad of cops would come charging out of the woods.

"This is far out, man," Peanut said, opening the car door. He then put the coke into a Piggly Wiggly bag we got from a store in Atlanta. After slipping the bag under his seat, he said, "That blow is worth way more than this Mustang. And now we've got both of them."

"No, what we have now is enough trouble to send us to prison for the rest of our lives," I said, gritting my teeth. "Peanut, you're talking through your ass. We don't know shit about selling this much coke. We need to fix this flat and get moving."

Twenty minutes later, I was breathing a little easier. We were on the road again. But the question now was, where to go. In Peanut's mind, finding the coke had changed everything.

"I say we head back to Miami," Peanut said excitedly. "I know a dealer who can buy the blow from us."

"Peanut, that *perico* and this car belongs to Vardon. Now that Vardon's dead, this stuff should go to his sister."

"Wise up, man," Peanut said. "Donny had us muleing that coke without telling us. If we'd gotten busted, it would have been our asses going to jail, not his."

"I don't care. We agreed to bring this car back – and that's what we should do."

"Shit, Cruiser," Peanut said, folding his arms across his chest. "Why do you always have to be such a goddam boy scout?"

"Look, man. We're in over our heads here," I said, trying to stay calm. "There's a chance whoever killed Vardon may have been after the coke that's under your seat right now. Have you thought about that?"

"No – but you don't know that for sure."

"No, I can't prove it. But that's only half of our problems, man. We're already caught up in a multiple murder and hauling drugs across state lines. If the cops catch us, how long do you think they'll put us away?"

Peanut scowled. "You don't have to go all Perry Mason on me. I see your point."

"So as long as we're holding that *perico*, we've got the heat and maybe even some killers on our ass. Let's not get greedy, man. This whole thing is a bag of snakes. The best thing we can do is give this car and the coke to Sheri Jean, get our thousand bucks and walk the hell away."

Peanut sighed. "Okay. Maybe you're right – but you're still a pussy."

# 10

**CRESTING A** hill, Fish's excitement dampened as she glimpsed a now-familiar sight: Paducah's water tower.

Pressing the pedal to the floor on the smoother stretch of road, she roared into the outskirts of town. There was no sign of the Mustang. From here, they could have gone anywhere.

Herring checked her watch. "*Fotze*," she said, under her breath. There was no time left for this bit of fun and games.

Her desire to take out the wits was more professional pride than anything else. If they went to the cops or the papers, so what? They'd help spread the word, which was just what the bosses wanted. The cops sure as hell wouldn't find any new evidence at the scene.

Besides wearing surgical gloves, she'd counted the empty slots in the Uzi's ammo clip and picked up every single shell casing before leaving Vardon's cabin. Once the weapon was in the river, any connection to her would be gone.

Erna peeled off the gloves, checked herself in the rearview mirror and reached for the makeup kit. She'd need to look presentable for her drive back home. Unkempt women stood out.

She was in her prime as a contract killer, no longer young but hardly old. A dishwater blond of average height and build, she could blend in anywhere – as long as the place was white.

Assured she was presentable, Fish turned the Fairmont north toward the truck stop on the highway back to Newport.

There was one item left to complete her contract.

The truck stop's parking lot was filling up with rigs as their drivers took a break for an evening meal. Fish parked next to a phone booth, walked inside, then looked up the number for the McCracken County sheriff.

"I want to report a murder," she said into the phone, then gave the dispatcher Vardon Jenkins' address.

"Who is this, please?" the dispatcher asked.

Erna hung up the phone, got into her car and headed home.

# 11

**"YOU THINK** this is it?" I asked Peanut, pulling into a drive-in burger joint.

The place had a long red roof stretching over a small diner and a couple of dozen parking spaces. Most of the spaces were filled with a mix of muscle cars and rusty pickups. An unlit neon sign by the road said: KunkleBurgers.

"Yeah," Peanut said, looking at Donny's map again. "KunkleBurgers is probably what Donny wrote here – but I won't swear to it."

"There's only one way to find out," I said, easing the Mustang into a parking space.

As I was leaning into the speaker, Peanut said, "Order me a double cheeseburger with everything."

"No. Let's just get cokes."

"Why can't I have a cheeseburger?"

"Someone will come out faster if we don't order food. We might have to try other restaurants if Sheri Jean's not here."

"Jesus, Cruiser. You're getting as bad as my mother," Peanut said, shaking his head.

After ordering the drinks, I had a chance to look around.

Every eye in the place was locked on us. Peanut noticed it too.

"Cruiser, we are definitely on the radar here."

"Yeah, I know."

The people staring at us from inside their cars looked like extras from West Side Story. The guys had slicked-back hair and rolled up collars - the chicks, ponytails and silky scarfs. It was like taking a time machine back to 1959. An odd thought struck me then. The only difference in styles between here and Miami was about ten years.

Our waitress showed up with two large drinks on a red plastic tray. The tag on her blouse said her name was Dot. She looked like Peanut's mom. "Y'all ain't from around here, are you?"

"We just got into town, Dot," I said, smiling. "We're trying to find someone. Do you know a Sheri Jean, by any chance?"

Dot looked at me for a moment, then said, "Either you boys are the dumbest car thieves on God's green earth or you're friends of Vardon Jenkins. 'Cause everybody around here knows this here's Vardon's Mustang. Now what do you boys want with Sheri Jean?"

My knees started to shake. I looked over at Peanut. His face was whiter than a movie star's smile. We now had a couple of dozen witnesses that put us in Vardon's car the day that he'd been killed. My first urge was to start the Mustang and get the hell out of there. But that was no use now. Maybe telling half the truth would save us.

"We just drove Vardon's car up from Miami for his cousin Donny," I said, trying to keep my knees still. "But nobody answered the door at Vardon's house. So now we're looking for Sheri Jean so we can give the car to her."

Dot broke into a smile. "Oh, Donny's still in Miami, is he?"

Jesus, I thought. How small is this town? "Yeah, that's right," I said. "He's got a job on a yacht now."

"Why, isn't that something?" Dot said.

"Yes, ma'am. And it's a big ol' boat, too. All purty and white," Peanut said, aping his mother's Georgia drawl.

"So can you tell us where to find Sheri Jean?" I asked, hoping Peanut hadn't laid the good-old-boy routine on too thick.

"Why, sure," Dot said sweetly. "Sheri Jean's off from work today. But I'll write down the directions to her place for you," she said and began scribbling on a paper napkin. After handing me the note, Dot looked at Peanut and said, "Before you go, let me get you some ice for that bump on your head, honey. It'll help with the swelling."

After Dot walked back toward the restaurant, I said, "Damn, Peanut. Dot's really nice."

"You shouldn't be surprised, Cruiser. Just because someone talks funny doesn't make them bad or stupid. *You* ought to know that better than anybody."

I thought about my dad's tortured English and hung my head. The little shit was right.

# 12

**BY THE** time we found Sheri Jean's place, it was getting close to dark.

"There it is," Peanut said pointing to a trailer park fronted by a plywood sign. THE ESTATES OF NOBLE PARK were hand-painted on the board in red letters. "Dot's directions say Sheri Jean lives in the fourth trailer on the left."

The look of this low-rent place worried me. "You think anybody who lives here's going to have a thousand bucks lying around?" I said, steering the Mustang onto a cracked driveway lined with slouching mobile homes.

"Hey, my mom says that in Georgia, moonshine millionaires live in places just like this to avoid the law."

"I sure hope your mom's right," I said as we pulled up to Sheri Jean's place. "Don't forget. We want to get this over with as fast as we can, man. It won't be long before somebody finds Vardon and his friends – and we want to be long gone before that shitstorm hits."

Peanut grabbed the Piggly Wiggly bag and we both walked to the trailer. I knocked on the metal door.

A brunette in her twenties appeared. Except for some acne scars, her face was pretty. But what really got my attention was the way she filled out her tube top and hip-hugging cutoffs.

"You must be Sheri Jean," I said with a smile. "Your cousin Donny asked us to return Vardon's car," I said nodding toward the Mustang behind me.

Sheri Jean took her time looking us over. "Y'all come inside," she said, a hint of promise in her voice.

Peanut and I sat on a sofa covered in what looked like pink fiberglass insulation. Sheri Jean sat across from us in a wicker chair. She crossed her slim legs and stroked her hair. "Seems you boys know my name," she told us. "But I can't say the same for you."

"I'm Cruiser and this is Peanut," I said. "Look, Sheri Jean, we tried to drop off the car at Vardon's place, but nobody came to the door. Donny told us we should bring the car to you if something like that happened. So, here we are," I said, holding out the car keys.

"Can I get you boys some ice water or something?" Sheri Jean asked, taking the keys. "Maybe some ice for that bump on your head?" she said to Peanut.

"No thanks. But there's another thing you need to know," I said, then cleared my throat. "We, uh... We found something under the car while we were fixing a flat. Show her, Peanut."

Peanut opened the Piggly Wiggly bag and held it so Sheri Jean could look inside. "We figured somebody around here might be looking for that," Peanut said, handing her the bag.

Sheri Jean put the bag in her lap and gave us a half smile. "That's real neighborly of you boys."

"There's something else, Sheri Jean," I said in my silkiest voice. "Donny told us we'd get a thousand dollars for bringing the car back."

Sheri Jean tapped her chin. "Hmmm. Will you boys excuse me for a minute?" she said, standing up.

"Sure."

Carrying the bag, she opened a door and walked into another room.

"What do you think's going on?" Peanut whispered.

"I'm hoping she went to get the bread," I whispered back.

A few minutes later, the door opened again and a guy entered the room. He had a military haircut and was about the size of a vending machine. I was relieved to see him smiling.

"You boys done right by our family," he said holding out his palm. "I'm Alvin."

I shook his hand and Peanut did the same. "Hi, Alvin. I'm Cruiser and this is Peanut."

"I hear Donny made you boys a promise."

"Yeah, man. A thousand bucks for bringing the car back."

"Sheri Jean," Alvin called out. "Would you bring my satchel in here, honey?" Then he looked at us and said, "In this family, we honor our word."

Sheri Jean walked in carrying an army shoulder bag and handed it to Alvin.

My jaw dropped as he unbuckled the bag and flipped it open. The thing was stuffed with stacks of neatly banded bills - with Ben Franklin's face on all of them. Alvin counted out ten bills and handed them to me. "Thank you, boys," he said.

"Believe me, man. We're glad this whole deal's done," I said, giving five Benjamins to Peanut and pocketing my share.

"You boys want something to drink?" Alvin asked.

"That's really nice of you, man. But me and Peanut need to split," I said standing up. "We could use a ride to the bus station, though."

"Sure. Sheri Jean can take you."

"You boys c'mon," Sheri Jean said, grabbing her purse and heading for the door. "We'll take my car. Driving Vardon's makes me nervous."

Getting our travel bags out of the Mustang's trunk, I felt a twinge of regret. I was glad we were heading home, but I had to admit, the trip had been a rush.

Moving the luggage had me vibing on some nostalgia, too.

The last time I'd used my travel bag was on the flight from Cuba to Miami as a kid. My dad had bought the blue PanAm carry-on for me as a gift. All stoked about the trip, I'd given the bag a name: Pancho.

As we followed Sheri Jean to her car, my mind kept pinballing between nostalgia, the urge to get out of town, and the dimples on Sheri Jean's back above those cutoffs.

# 13

**SHERI JEAN** stopped her Valiant in front of the Paducah bus station, a concrete bunker about the size of a two-car garage with a picture of a skinny running dog on the wall.

"I'm sorry to see y'all leave so soon. We don't get too many hippie boys around here," she said with a smile, touching my hair.

"Thanks for the ride," I said, grabbing my bag and sliding out of the car.

"Yeah, thanks," Peanut echoed, getting out of the back seat.

"Well, I expect you boys might have some time to kill before your bus leaves," Sheri Jean said, making sure our eyes met. "I'll be in the lounge at the motel across the street for a while," she said, nodding toward the Hickory Tree Inn. "Maybe we can have a few beers and shoot some pool."

"How long you think we'll have to wait?" I asked. Her invitation sounded temping. But getting out of town sounded better.

She laughed softly. "This is a small town, darlin'. You'll see."

After Sheri Jean drove away, I followed Peanut through the glass door into the station. The small room smelled like mold, sweat and desperation. An old man in a wrinkled suit was slumped in one of the plastic chairs bolted to the wall, a cardboard suitcase by his feet. He was the only passenger in the place.

The old man's face lit up when we walked in. "Are you Billy Ray?" he asked Peanut, adjusting thick, yellow-tinted glasses.

"No, sir. Sorry," Peanut said, taken by surprise.

The old guy's face sagged. "Sorry to bother, y'all."

"Hey, I'm sure Billy Ray's coming soon," I said, wondering how long the poor guy had been waiting.

At the ticket counter, a sleepy-looking bald guy was reading *Grit* magazine. "Excuse me," I said. "When does the next bus to Miami leave?"

The bald guy sighed and slowly closed the magazine. "Y'all give me a minute," he said and began looking through the schedule like he was afraid of spraining an eyeball if he read too fast. Peanut started pacing and I began to fidget. An hour seemed to pass before the clerk finally raised his head and spoke. "Next bus to Miami leaves at ten-twenty tomorrow morning."

"What? Are you kidding me?" I said, stomach suddenly tight. Somebody was bound to find the pile of bodies at Vardon's house before then.

"You boys look like you're from the city," the bald guy said – and it didn't sound like a compliment. "Things move a little slower around here."

# 14

**THE SKY** was the color of grape jelly when we walked out of the bus station.

"What do you want to do?" Peanut said.

"We've got to try something else, man. We can't stay here until tomorrow."

I looked around and saw a phone booth. Walking toward it, I said "Maybe they've got an airport."

Unable to get into the booth with my bag, I put Pancho down by the door.

As Peanut hovered outside, I opened the Paducah Yellow Pages and began flipping feverishly through the book. My shoulders slumped when I found the single airport listing. "It's for private planes only," I said, stepping out of the booth.

"Goddam this Podunk town!" Peanut said, then kicked Pancho.

A flash of rage came over me and I shoved him. Peanut flew about six feet before he skidded along the pavement for a few more.

"What the fuck is your problem, Cruiser?" he yelled, getting to his feet, fists clenched.

"I've had that bag since I was a kid in Cuba." I couldn't bring myself to tell him I'd given it a name.

Instead of coming at me, Peanut picked up Pancho and handed it to me.

"Hey. I get it, man," Peanut said, then opened the

zipper on his own bag. From the bottom, he pulled out a green plastic soldier throwing a grenade. "This is the only toy I still have from Georgia."

We both stood there for a while. Then Peanut said, "We've got to get out of here, Cruiser."

"Okay, wait. I've got another idea," I said, trying to stay positive. "Let's buy a car. We've got enough bread between us."

"Shit, man. I don't want to blow all our money."

"Fine, I'm sure your five hundred bucks will buy a lot of cigarettes in prison. Oh, wait," I said sneering. "You'll probably spend most of it on a lawyer first."

"All right, smartass. I see your point," Peanut said. "Can we get a convertible?"

We spent the next fifteen minutes calling all four car dealers in the Paducah Yellow Pages. None of them answered the phone.

"Mom says it's the same way in Waycross, man," Peanut said. "They roll up the streets after—"

Peanut clammed up and locked his eyes on something behind me. I turned and saw a black and white sheriff's cruiser pull into the bus station parking lot.

My heart started to thump. I was ready to fly out of there.

Peanut read my mind. "Don't run," he whispered. "He's just bird-dogging."

Sure enough, the deputy stared at us for a minute, then drove away.

"That was close," I said, finally breathing again.

"Man, we've got to blow this place," Peanut said. "This is the main road out of town. Let's hitch a ride."

I shook my head. "We try hitchhiking around here at

night and we might as well put a bull's-eye on our shirts, man. One of these good 'ol boys will use us for target practice.

"Well, what the hell are we going to do then?"

"I don't know, man," I said, rubbing my face. "My brain is dry."

We both stood there for a moment, staring at the pavement.

Then Peanut snapped his fingers. "I've got an idea, man," he said, starting to smile. "Sheri Jean said she'd be hanging out in that lounge, right?" he said, pointing to the motel across the street.

"Yeah. So what? You want to drink some beer and play pool until the heat picks us up?"

"No, man," Peanut said, grinning slyly. "I saw the way Sheri Jean checked you out, Cruiser. You could hit it off with her and get us a ride out of town."

"Hmm. You may have something there, man," I said, rubbing my chin. "All right. I guess I can take one for the team. We sure as hell don't have much to lose."

15

**"THERE'S SHERI** Jean," Peanut said as we entered the Hickory Tree Lounge.

She was on a chrome stool at the end of the bar with three fat guys in golf shirts hovering nearby like flies around spilled syrup. Seeing us walk in, Sheri Jean stood and started toward us. The fat guys hung their heads and stopped sucking in their guts.

"You boys gonna be around long?" Sheri Jean said as we met near the center of the club.

"Enough time for a few beers," I said, not wanting to tip my hand.

Peanut handed me his travel bag. "Hey, I'll get the beer. You two grab a booth," he said, winking at me.

I threw our bags across the booth from Sheri Jean and sat down next to her. "I was expecting to see a lot of John Deere caps and overalls in here," I said to Sheri Jean, nodding toward the preppy-looking fat guys.

"This place mostly caters to traveling salesmen. It's too fancy for the locals. They hang out down the road at Mousie's."

Peanut came back with a couple of beers and put them down in front of us. "I'm going to shoot some pool," he said and left us alone.

"Seems like you know this place pretty well," I said.

"It's nice to have a classy joint in town. But the sales guys in here can get a little pushy."

"You can't blame them. I mean, a gorgeous chick like you is always going to draw a crowd," I said, giving her a high beam smile.

"Mighty nice of you to say that, Cruiser," she said, smiling back.

We chatted for a while, edging closer to each other as we sipped our beers. Our shoulders touched, then our knees. There was no confusing Sheri Jean's vibe.

I looked into her eyes. "You know, that smile of yours could make the moon feel jealous."

"Cruiser, I believe you could charm the red off a tomato."

"So, how am I doing with *you?*"

"Mmmm. I'd say it's working, darlin'," she said, her voice turning sultry. "I've got a lid of Columbian in my car. You want to go out for a toke?"

# 16

**THE RED** lights of the cruiser's bubble gum machine swirled through the tree branches lining the narrow gravel path. Seated beside the sheriff's deputy at the wheel, Special Agent Jack Brill straightened his tie and lit a Pall Mall.

Arriving at the crime scene, Brill saw a gray two-story cabin with three vehicles and another squad car parked nearby. A lanky man in a sheriff's uniform stood by the door.

Hiking his belt over a bulging paunch, Brill stepped out of the cruiser.

"Are the bodies still inside?" Brill asked.

The sheriff nodded respectfully. "Yessir. We left everything intact for you, Mister Brill."

"Let's go in," Brill said, stepping through the door.

After 11 years as an FBI agent, Brill was used to being kowtowed to by local cops. He wasn't fooled, however. These guys could turn on you faster than a wino going through a bottle of Ripple.

Once they reached the bodies, Brill took a long pull from his cigarette and slowly scanned the room. "Fill me in, Sheriff. From the beginning," he said.

"My office got a John Doe tip about the murders around five this afternoon. We tried to trace the call but came up empty. When me and my deputy got here, we found the bodies. Coroner says they was killed no more than two hours earlier. Them amplifiers there was still wailing till we cut the juice." The sheriff waved his hand across the room. "Don't look like nothing was stolen. The house wasn't tossed. No shell casings. But here's the kicker... we found two kilos of cocaine in a bedroom closet."

Brill raised his eyebrows but said nothing.

"This whole mess smells like an organized crime hit to me, Mr. Brill. Most likely, the Dixie Mafia. That's why I called your office."

"What made you think organized crime was involved?" Brill asked. "One of the guys in this band could have been banging someone's wife."

The sheriff glanced at his shoes. "Word around town is that the owner of the house, Vardon Jenkins, had started pushing a little dope."

"And you didn't investigate Jenkins based on this information?"

"Here's the thing, Mr. Brill. People in a small town like to gossip. I don't have time to go around chasing rumors," the sheriff said, shuffling his feet. "Besides, Vardon and the Viceroys play at the county fair every year. These boys are real popular around here. You know what I mean?"

Brill knew exactly what the sheriff meant. When you're an elected lawman, you're inclined to look the other way when the voters who put you in office are fond of a criminal. And the FBI makes a perfect scapegoat to take the blame when the criminal is finally busted.

"I'm starting to get the picture here, Sheriff," Brill said, rubbing his jowls. "You think the Dixie Mafia wanted to squash a new pissant dealer on their turf... and send a message to anyone else who might have similar ambitions."

"I'd say that's just about right, Mr. Brill."

Brill took another drag from the cigarette. "Got any

leads on suspects?"

"Like I said, everybody around here loves these boys."

Brill sighed. The sheriff had succeeded in tossing this porcupine into his lap. With a multiple murder under these circumstances, he had no choice but to take the case. "I'll get our forensics people over here to sort out the physical evidence. If the killers were pros, I doubt my people will have much to go on. Get your office busy locating next of kin. We'll want to talk to all of them for motives."

"We could set up roadblocks on the main roads out of town," the sheriff offered.

"Save your manpower. If the killers called and tipped you off, they're long gone," Brill said.

"How do you want to handle the press? The local paper follows the morgue sheets. They're sure to have some questions about four bodies full of bullet holes."

"I don't want anyone except the killers to know the details of these murders," Brill said. "If any reporters ask, tell them we'll be notifying next of kin. Nothing else."

"No mention of the drugs?"

"Not a word."

"Having nothing for the press won't make us look too good."

"I'm not here to help your reelection, Sheriff. I'm here to solve this crime," Brill said. "Have your deputies quietly ask around about any strangers seen in the area. Tomorrow we'll start working the next of kin. Meantime, I'll need a place to stay – for one night at least."

The three-hour drive from his office in Louisville wouldn't let Brill commute to this case. Brill silently cursed his luck. This crap didn't happen to the ass-kissers at the Bureau who got the plum assignments.

His face taut, the sheriff said, "I'll have one of my boys set you up with a motel room, Mister Brill."

# 17

**THE NIGHT** was getting chilly. So we rolled up the windows after getting in the backseat of Sheri Jean's sedan. She reached under the seat, got out her stash, and fired up a joint.

"You ever try shot gunning?" she asked.

"What's that?" I asked, thinking she might be into something kinky.

"Trust me. You're going to love it."

Sheri Jean put the lit end of the joint between her teeth, put her hands on my face and pulled me toward her until our lips were touching. Then she blew the smoke into my mouth. I inhaled, taking in a monster hit. By the time she pulled away, I was buzzing hard.

"Far out," I said, my vision getting blurry.

"Okay, now you do me," Sheri Jean said, handing me the joint.

It was goddam sexy, let me tell you. And the high – my God, it kicked your ass. By the time we finished the joint, the windows were steamed up and clothes were flying. I lost track of time.

The next thing I remember clearly was Sheri Jean laying back and saying, "Darlin', that hair of yours ain't the only thing that's long."

I was feeling pretty good about then – until I remembered why I'd come to see Sheri Jean.

"Maybe we could do this again in a motel," I said.

"Someplace in another town where not everybody knows you."

"Yeah, that would be nice," she said, still half-baked. "But there's something I should tell you, darlin'," she murmured. "That money Alvin gave you – it's no good."

"What do mean, no good?"

"Alvin sold some reefer to a biker gang and they paid him with counterfeit money. Wasn't much he could do about it either. No way Alvin's gonna muscle a biker gang. So when you came along, Alvin was happier than a pig in shit to unload the bad paper on you."

I swallowed hard. This was not good. As I laid there, wondering what to do, I nearly levitated off the car seat when someone tapped on the window. I couldn't see who it was through the foggy glass.

"Sheri Jean," a man's voice outside the car said, "Alvin just called for you."

"Tell him I'm in the ladies' room and I'll be there in a minute, Carl," she called out. Then she leaned close to my ear and whispered, "It's the bartender. You wait here, darlin'."

I was amazed how fast she got dressed and left the car.

First thing I did was roll down the windows. If there was a chance her husband might show up, the steamed-up glass would be a dead giveaway.

Just as I was putting on my shoes, Sheri Jean got in behind the wheel.

"I'm sorry to do this, darlin', but you've got to get out of the car – right now. Alvin's coming this way and if he catches us together, there's gonna be hell to pay."

I've been around the block enough to know when to move fast. I stepped out into the parking lot with one of my shoes still in my hand.

Sheri Jean spoke to me through the window. "The last bus out of Paducah leaves at eleven-fifteen every night. You boys best be on it."

"Look. I'm sorry to come between you and your husband."

"Husband? Alvin's my cousin," she said before speeding away.

# 18

**IT WAS** after midnight when Fish pulled into the parking lot of a roadside diner. The place was closed, the only light coming from a phonebooth next to the one-time railroad car.

The location was perfect Erna thought, getting out of the car. With the contract complete, she'd need to call her client and arrange the dead drop back in Newport for the second half of her pay.

After dialing the number, Fish was surprised by her employer's response.

"TV ain't had nothing on the hit. We got people up there watching, you know," the southern fried voice said.

Erna rubbed the bridge of her nose. "I can't figure why it hasn't made the news," she said into the receiver. "I tipped off the sheriff's office by phone right after I finished the job."

"Your work don't do us no good unless any other twerps like Vardon Jenkins gets the message to stay the hell out of our business."

"I'm sure it's just a matter of time before the story breaks."

"That's not good enough. You ain't gonna see a nickel of that other five grand until we see something in the news. We're paying you top dollar. Earn it," the mob boss said before hanging up.

"*Depp,*" Fish muttered as she got into the car and headed back toward Paducah.

# 19

**RUNNING INTO** the lounge through the back door, I looked at the Schlitz beer clock above the bar. It was just after eleven. Peanut was bent over the pool table, lining up a shot. I put my pinkies in the corners of my mouth and whistled. Peanut looked up, pissed that I'd made him miss. But when he saw the look on my face, he put down the cue stick and started toward me.

"We've got to split – now," I said, tossing him his bag. After I grabbed Pancho, we booked through the front door.

"What's going on, man?" Peanut said after we were outside.

"We need to get to the bus station. C'mon," I said, breaking into a run. "I'll tell you on the way."

Sprinting beside me, Peanut said, "What happened with Sheri Jean?"

"We got it on. But now Alvin's headed this way," I said panting. "Did you spend any of his money?"

"Yeah, I bought a round for the sales guys – to keep them from kicking your ass over Sheri Jean."

"The money Alvin gave us – it's counterfeit, man."

"Tell me you're kidding, Cruiser."

"Wish I was, man," I said as we reached the bus station. "Give me the change from the hundred."

"Why?" Peanut asked as we stood outside the door.

"That's the money we're going to use to buy our bus tickets."

"Why don't we break another hundred?"

"Because the feds follow counterfeit money, man. They'll know where we're going if we buy our bus tickets with it."

"Where are we going?"

"Wherever the eleven-fifteen bus is headed."

# 20

**PEANUT AND** I were still sucking wind as we got on the bus. The driver gave us a hard look as he punched our tickets. I barely noticed. My attention was focused out the windows. There was no sign of Alvin or the heat. Relieved, we started down the aisle.

The bus was about half full, with everyone near the front. I nodded for Peanut to follow and headed for the empty seats in the back. It didn't take us long to turn around.

Peanut scrunched his nose as we got near the restroom at the rear of the bus. "Man, somebody needs to check that shithole for a body," he said.

We found a pair of seats as far as we could from the stink and tossed our bags in the overhead rack. An older guy across the aisle said, "Now you know why they call this bus line the Dirty Dog." He had chestnut skin and a pork-pie hat.

"No shit," I said, sliding in next to Peanut.

"Too *much* shit," he said chuckling.

I nodded but looked away, still too spun up to laugh.

When the bus driver finally closed the door, turned off the interior lights and pulled away from the station, my paranoia dropped a notch. The passengers got quiet and hid their eyes from each other, trying to find some privacy in the close quarters.

A few miles down the road, the lights of Paducah disappeared behind us as the bus entered the pitch black of the countryside. I laid my head back and closed my eyes, relaxing for the first time today. After all the shit we'd been through, all I wanted was to put my brain in neutral and veg out for a while. What I got instead was a whisper fight from Peanut.

"Hey, man" he hissed. "If it didn't matter where we were going, why didn't we take the first bus out of Paducah to begin with?"

"You were there too, Einstein," I whispered back, feeling stupid but not wanting to admit it. "You could have said let's go someplace besides Miami."

"Okay, so now we're going to Detroit. What the hell are we going to do there?"

"Not go to jail, for one thing," I said. "Now shut up and let me sleep. We can figure things out later."

# 21

**BEHIND THE** wheel of the Fairmont, Fish rubbed her eyes and popped another benny. There would be no sleep for her tonight. She'd need to drive non-stop to be back in Paducah by morning.

Erna already had a play in mind to find out why the county sheriff had clammed up about the hit. She'd even brought along the right outfit – an avocado pantsuit.

She liked to be prepared. On most jobs she took along two suitcases: one for clothes, the other for weapons. Her motto when packing for a hit was: "Maybe I should bring that too."

Despite her diligence, making a living was getting harder all the time.

Her line of work had been much easier until that fucking Bobby Kennedy had broken up the Newport syndicate in '61. Until then, the Kentucky town across the river from Cincinnati was known as Sin City.

The Cleveland bosses had owned the place. Everyone was in their pocket: the casino owners, the politicians, the police, even the pimps. Newport's nightclubs had brought in stars like Frank Sinatra and Dean Martin. The whorehouses were first-rate. Booze was cheap and plentiful. Hits were simple and paid well. Life was good.

But Kennedy's do-gooders in the DOJ had driven all the gambling, dealing and whorehouses from Newport to Las Vegas.

She'd tried living in Vegas for a while. But unlike most contractors who were Sicilians, she was German. The heat gave her a rash – and scratching an uncontrollable itch could be fatal for someone in her line of work.

So she'd stuck it out in Newport where she'd been brought by her parents from Dusseldorf after the war when she was eight.

Now, she worked for cornpone capos who chewed tobacco and made their bones running moonshine up and down these hills – bosses without any class at all.

Fish shook her head, trying to chase away those thoughts. She needed to focus on the job at hand. This wasn't the time for regrets.

# 22

**GETTING ANY** real sleep on the bus had been impossible.

Every couple of hours, the interior lights would come on as we stopped at another little town. Passengers would take down their bags and shuffle off. Then new ones would get on and stow their luggage. The string of rude awakenings was pure torture. A book I'd once read said the KGB did the same thing to interrogate prisoners.

A quiet jail cell where I could get some sleep was starting to sound pretty damn good.

The sun was creeping over the trees when the bus pulled into the terminal at a town called Beach Groove or something. The driver stood and faced the passengers. "We'll be stopping here for breakfast," he said, then looked directly at Peanut and me. "Anyone not back aboard in exactly thirty minutes is getting left behind."

From the look on the driver's face, it was clear freaks weren't very common on his bus – or welcome. Shrugging it off, we stepped outside to a rude surprise.

The weather had turned cold.

After eating and taking care of business in the terminal, Peanut and I slipped into an alley behind the station and fired up a joint.

Hunched against the chill, Peanut took a hit and passed me the doob. "Enjoy it, man," he said, "This is the last of our stash."

"Bummer," I said, taking a toke.

"You want to go all the way to Detroit or get off somewhere else and take another bus to Miami?"

Before I could answer, we heard footsteps. Peanut glanced around the corner. "Somebody's coming," he whispered.

I pinched out the joint and slipped it into my pocket before exhaling a cloud of smoke.

The guy from the bus in the porkpie hat walked around the corner of the building. He sniffed the air and smiled. "The song is over, but the melody lingers on."

"What?" Peanut said, looking confused.

The guy in the hat gave us a wink. "Y'all seen anybody around here smoking reefer? 'Cause if you did, I'd ask them to join me in a toke," he said, then pulled a tidily rolled joint from his coat pocket. As he lit it with a well-worn Zippo, I noticed his left hand only had a thumb and forefinger. "Care for a taste?" he said, handing Peanut the doob.

"Thanks, man. Don't mind if I do," Peanut said, toking up.

"My name's Chester, gentlemen," he said, touching the brim of his hat.

"I'm Cruiser and that little shit with a face full of weed is Peanut."

"Nice to meet you both."

"Where are you headed, Chester?" I asked as Peanut handed me the joint.

"Got a gig in Detroit," he said, pronouncing it DEEtroit.

"You're a musician?"

Chester nodded. "Trumpet's my axe, son."

"Far out," I said before taking a hit.

"Look, boys. I try to mind my own business, but I couldn't help noticing that y'all look to be in some kind of trouble."

Peanut coughed. "No, we're not in any trouble," he said a little too quickly.

"Huh," Chester said shrugging. "I must've misunderstood all that looking around and whispering. 'Cause if I was to guess, I'd say you boys might be draft dodgers headed for Canada."

I exhaled and shook my head. "No, man. I was three-twenty-one in the lottery."

"And I was two-eighty-seven," Peanut added.

"Uh, huh," Chester said, looking skeptical. "Well, if you boys *was* draft dodgers, I'd tell you to go on down to Plum Street when you get to Detroit," he said. "That's where the hippies hang out. There's folks down there that helps draft dodgers get across the border."

"Thanks for the scoop, Chester," I said, handing him the joint.

"Look, I ain't against fighting for my country. I was in the Seven-Sixty-First during the war. But all we're doing over there in Vietnam is wasting lives – and it's a goddam shame," he said. Then he took a hit and handed Peanut the joint. "You boys take care, now."

Watching Chester walk away, I realized he'd given us two gifts: an extra doob for our stash and maybe a way out of this mess.

**23**

**THE TELEPHONE** on the motel room's nightstand rang.

In boxers and a wifebeater, Jack Brill picked up the handset without getting out of bed. "Yeah?" he said, rubbing his eyes.

"I'll be there in twenty minutes, Mr. Brill," he heard the sheriff say.

"Got it," Brill muttered as he returned the handset to its cradle.

He walked to the room's tiny desk and stowed a half empty fifth of Jack Daniels and the latest issue of *True Detective* magazine into his valise.

*A-jack-and-a-jack* was Brill's private code for the habit: one jack from the bottle, the other from the scantily clad women in the magazine.

At 36, Brill had never married. He buried himself in his work to blot out those yearnings. But at night, away from the daytime distractions, he retreated to his routine. By morning, the shame and loneliness usually morphed into anger. There was always a perp to collar – and assholes at the office eager to see him fail.

As Brill entered the bathroom, he was surprised not to have heard from Henry last night. That was unusual. But Brill was sure Henry would speak to him.

By the time the sheriff arrived, Brill had showered, strapped on his Colt Detective Special and donned a black polyester suit. Polyester traveled well.

Balding and overweight, Brill knew he didn't fit the suave look of an FBI agent like the one Efrem Zimbalist Jr. played on television. Anyway, he preferred Jack Webb's bad-ass attitude from Dragnet – and he'd need it today.

Questioning the next of kin was routine in most murder cases. But Brill wanted to be sure a goober-town sheriff queasy about pissing off voters didn't pitch softballs and miss something.

As Brill slid into the passenger's seat of the cruiser, the sheriff handed him a small paper bag. "I thought you might like some breakfast."

"Thanks," Brill answered. Opening the bag, he found a pair of oily pastries. "What's this?"

"Rhubarb fried pies. Missus Fugate at the Dew Drop Inn makes the best in town."

Brill took a bite. "Not bad," he said, scarfing down the rest.

"Brought you some coffee, too," the sheriff said, passing him a cardboard cup.

Brill took the cup and nodded in thanks. After downing a slug, he grimaced and said, "Stationhouse brew?"

"How did you know?"

"Tastes like horse piss everywhere I go."

The sheriff tried to feign a smile but came up short. "By the way, I got a call this morning you should know about," he said, pulling out of the motel parking lot. "A night club owner here in town found some bad paper in the till. Says his bartender was passed a bogus hundred last night by a pair of hippies."

Brill felt his pulse rise. "Were these hippies seen anywhere else?"

"One of my deputies saw a pair of longhairs at the bus

station last night. I'm still waiting to hear from my other boys asking around."

"Shame to hear that kind of commie vermin is spreading out here from their shitholes in the cities."

"You got that right, Mr. Brill. And passing bad paper, too."

"I don't think this has anything to do with our murders, though."

The sheriff shrugged. "The hippie thing could be a disguise."

"Professional hit men don't travel by bus. Counterfeiters don't either. It doesn't add up."

"I don't know, Mr. Brill. It's damned clever if you think on it."

Brill stared at the passing countryside for a moment. "Have one of your men get me the schedule for the buses leaving town."

"I can tell you part of that myself," the sheriff said with a grin. "Last bus leaves Paducah at eleven-fifteen every night."

"Where does it go?"

"It goes to Detroit – eventually," the sheriff explained. "But it stops at damned near every little burg in between. The killers could get off at one of those towns and light out for hell-knows where."

Brill rubbed his jowls. "So maybe it's not that crazy to think a pair of hit men might blow town on a bus."

"Maybe," the sheriff said, nodding.

They rode in silence for the next few miles until the sheriff steered the cruiser into a trailer park. "This here's our first stop. Vardon's sister," he said, pointing to a dingy doublewide. An old pickup, a battered sedan and a shiny new Mustang were parked in front of the mobile home.

After knocking on the metal door, Brill heard scuffling and thumps inside.

The sheriff knocked again. Still no answer.

Following a third knock, a brunette in curlers and a bath robe opened the door a few inches and peered outside.

"Sheri Jean Jenkins?" the sheriff asked.

Sheri Jean's eyes darted from side to side. "Yeah?"

"I'm sorry to inform you that your brother Vardon is dead."

For an instant, Sherri Jean seemed relieved. Then, her eyes widened. "Oh, my Lord! What happened?"

"He was shot at his home yesterday along with the members of his band," the sheriff said, nodding his head in sympathy.

"Do you know who did it?"

"That's why we're here," the sheriff said, then gestured toward his companion. "This is Agent Brill of the FBI. We'd like to ask some questions to help us find the culprits. Can we come in?"

Sheri Jean's hand trembled as she touched her cheek. "The house is a mess, Sheriff. Can you come back another time?"

"I'm sorry, Sheri Jean. This is urgent," the sheriff answered with a soft smile.

Brill stepped closer to the door. In a cold voice, he said, "Are you hiding something, Miss Jenkins?"

"N-n-no, sir," she stuttered.

"Then a messy house is no reason to halt the wheels of justice, is it?"

Sheri Jean glanced back into the trailer, then turned

her gaze back to the lawmen and opened the door. "Y'all come in," she said, waving them inside.

# 24

**AS THE** lawmen stepped inside, Sheri Jean looked around the trailer's cramped living room, hoping she'd gotten all the dope out of sight.

After seeing the cop car in the driveway, she'd barely had time to wake up Alvin and get him to hide under the bed – along with his bad money and the coke. In the living room, she'd swept the conglomeration of drugs on the coffee table onto a throw rug, then folded the rug and shoved it into a cabinet under the sink.

"Please sit down," she said nervously, waving toward the pink couch she'd ordered from Monkey Wards.

While Sheri Jean perched herself on the edge of a wicker chair, the men settled awkwardly on the low couch, their knees nearly touching their chins.

"When was the last time you saw your brother," the sheriff asked.

Sheri Jean tapped a finger on her lips. "Let me think... Would have been last week. He came by KunkleBurgers for lunch. That's where I work."

The sheriff nodded. "Did you see your brother very often?"

"Well, not a lot really. We wasn't all that close."

"Did your brother have any enemies, Miss Jenkins?" the agent asked.

"No. No, sir. Everybody likes Vardon."

"I understand your brother played in a band," the agent

said. "Did he have any other kind of business on the side?"

"If he did, I sure didn't know nothing about it," she said, shaking her head.

"You're here alone?" the agent asked.

"Yes, sir."

Brill's eyes narrowed. "There are three vehicles parked outside. Care to explain that?"

"Oh, that? Well, sure. You see, um... my cousin Alvin leaves his pickup here sometimes when one of his friends drives him to work. They save on gas that way."

"And the Mustang? Is that yours?"

Sheri Jean's cheeks flushed. "Well, actually. That's Vardon's," she said, her voice fading to a whisper.

"I'm confused, Miss Jenkins. You say you're not close to your brother and haven't seen him in a week. Yet, his car is parked outside your home."

"I can explain that, sir. Really, I can," Sheri Jean said, wringing her hands. "It's kind of a long story."

"We have time."

"Okay. Well, we have a cousin named Donny who borrowed Vardon's car. Then Donny, on account of he had something else to do, asked some fellas to bring the car back and they brought it here."

"Miss Jenkins, there's a lot more we need to know," the agent said, his voice hardening. "Who are these men who returned the car to you? When were they here? Why did they return the car to you instead of Vardon?"

Sheri Jean's mind raced. There was no way she could deny knowing Cruiser and Peanut. The bartender at the Hickory Tree had seen her with the hippies. Hell, Carl had even caught her shucking oysters with Cruiser in her car. Unless she came up with a good story, she could go to jail.

Sheri Jean covered her face and began to sob. "I'm sorry. I should have told y'all this sooner," she said. "I'm just really scared, hearing that my brother was killed and all. I thought those goons would come after me if I snitched."

"All right. Calm down, Miss Jenkins," the agent said softening his tone. "Tell us about the men who brought your brother's car."

"They talked like a couple of big-city thugs. Said their names was Cruiser and Peanut," she said, dabbing her nose. "They came here yesterday and said our cousin Donny asked them to bring Vardon's Mustang back from Miami. It all sounded kinda fishy to me. Now I can see what happened. They stole the car from Vardon's house after they killed him."

"Why did they bring the car to you?"

"They wanted money," she said. "A thousand dollars."

"Did you give them the money?"

She shook her head. "Where would I get that kind of dough?"

The sheriff leaned forward and said, "Nothing was stolen at Vardon's house. If these men killed your brother, why would they come to you for money?"

"Never mind that, Miss Jenkins," the agent said, giving the sheriff a sour look. "Can you describe these men?"

"They both had long hair. You know, like hippies."

"One of my boys saw a pair of hippies last night down at the—"

The agent touched the sheriff's arm, cutting him off. "They had long hair. How else would you describe them?"

"Cruiser's kinda tall and good-looking. Peanut's a runt. But he looks real mean. Had a bruise on his head like he'd been in a fight."

"Last names?"

"They didn't give them, and I didn't ask."

"If Vardon's car is here, how did they leave?"

"They asked me to take them to the bus station. So I did."

"What time?"

Sheri Jean paused for a moment. "I wanted them out of here as soon as I could. So I drove them to the bus station just after they got here, around seven-thirty."

"And that was the last time you saw them?"

Sheri Jean felt her face redden. This was going to be tricky – especially with Alvin in the bedroom and able to hear every word. "After I took them to the bus station, I stopped at the Hickory Tree to play some pool. Cruiser and Peanut showed up at the lounge after a while, on account of their bus not leaving for a few hours," she said, then added, "The bus station's just across the street."

"The manager at the Hickory Tree told me two hippies passed his bartender a counterfeit hundred last night," said the sheriff. "You know anything about that?"

Sheri Jean forced herself not to smile. This was the break that might keep her out of jail. "Well, now that you say that, I recollect them two bragging at the lounge about their fake money, Sheriff. Said they had themselves a lot of it."

"That makes no sense, Miss Jenkins," the agent answered. "Why would they have asked you for money to return the car if they didn't need it?"

Sheri Jean shrugged. "They wanted clean money, I suppose," she said. "Their fake bill must not have been too good if the lounge manager spotted it so fast." Sheri Jean said the last part good and loud so dumbass Alvin would

be sure to get the message.

The lawmen looked at each other for a moment, then nodded. "I think we're done here for now, Miss Jenkins," the agent said.

"One of my deputies will stop by soon. We'll need you to come to the morgue and identify the body," the sheriff said as they rose to their feet. "I'm sorry for the loss of your brother, Sheri Jean."

# 25

**BRILL FELT** a little queasy as the cruiser lurched right at the bottom of a curve. Riding on this roller coaster country road was unsettling his stomach – and they had three more next of kin visits to make.

Brill kept it to himself, though. Complaining about nausea was a sign of weakness he didn't dare show in front of the sheriff.

As they crested another steep hill, the cruiser's radio squawked to life.

"Star One, this is Star Four."

The sheriff picked up the handset. "This is Star One. Come on, Star Four."

"Sheriff, I'm here with Dot at KunkleBurgers. She says two hippies was over here yesterday and they was driving Vardon Jenkins' Mustang. Over."

The sheriff's eyebrows rose. "Ask Dot what time she saw the hippies. Over."

After a moment, the deputy replied. "Dot says around six of the evening, Sheriff. Over."

"Copy that, Star Four. Good work, Bobby. Star One out," the sheriff said, replacing the handset. Turning to face Brill, the sheriff said, "That sighting of the hippies came after we got the John Doe call, Mr. Brill. And it backs up Sheri Jean's story. Cruiser and Peanut was at KunkleBurgers right before Sheri Jean said they come to her place."

Brill closed his eyes, trying to ignore the undulating landscape. "Sheri Jean's story had more holes than a Chicago pool hall."

"Maybe so. But those two have got to be our hit men, Mr. Brill."

"I'm not convinced."

"You don't think some hillbilly mobsters would be smart enough to pose as hippies?"

"On the contrary. I think they'd be way too smart to pull such a stupid stunt."

"Nothing else makes any sense," the sheriff said, shaking his head.

Brill closed his eyes, trying to quell the nausea. He was certain the guys Sheri Jean called Cruiser and Peanut were not professional killers. But what were two hippies doing at the scene of a multiple homicide?

The taste of rhubarb fried pie rose suddenly in Brill's throat. He managed to get the window open before hurling his breakfast into the countryside.

"You okay, Mr. Brill?" the sheriff asked, bringing the cruiser to a stop.

"I'll be fine," he said, wiping his mouth on his sleeve.

"These back roads can do that to folks that ain't used to them," the sheriff said. "Maybe them rhubarb pies didn't help none. That's on me," he said. "I'll take you back to your motel and let you rest for a bit and get cleaned up. Then we'll start up again after lunch. I'll go the long way around next time and take a flatter route."

# 26

**"I TOLD** the sheriff you were here, Miss Cole. He's on his way back. You can go on into his office and wait," the secretary said, pointing toward the door.

From the guest chair in the sheriff's office, Fish scanned the place as she waited for the lawman to appear. The wall behind the sheriff's desk looked like a saint's shrine.

A yard-high six-pointed sheriff's badge was flanked by the flags of the U.S. and Kentucky in each corner. Between the flags, the wall was covered in gold-framed photos of the sheriff being interviewed on television, testifying in court, and making arrests. Alongside the photos were framed newspaper articles featuring his exploits, and the blown-up cover of *Western Kentucky* magazine with the tall lawman in a Smokey the Bear hat posing by a cruiser.

Fish had read this guy right. The most dangerous place to be in McCracken County was between this sheriff and a press camera.

When the lawman entered the room, Fish stood and said, "Good morning, Sheriff. Thanks for taking the time to see me."

"Always glad to help the press get out the word to the people I'm sworn to protect, Miss Cole," he said, gesturing for her to sit down.

"That's why I'm here, sir," she said, straightening the jacket of the pantsuit she'd chosen for this ruse.

"How can I serve the readers of the *Louisville Post?*" he

said, leaning on the edge of his desk.

"Sheriff, I know you're sitting on a big story. I'm here to help you get the word out."

The sheriff cocked his head. "I don't rightly know what you're talking about."

"I can't reveal my sources, but we both know there's been a multiple murder in this county. Yet your office hasn't gone public with any information."

The sheriff 's eyebrows rose. "Who have you been talking to?"

"That's confidential, sir. I protect my sources. And I'll protect your privacy as well."

"I'm sorry but I have no comment on any ongoing investigations, Miss Cole," he said, raising his palm.

"I understand, Sheriff. You can't risk putting out details of a crime that tip your hand to the culprits. I get that," she said. "But we can help each other here if you're willing to go off-the-record."

"What do you have in mind?" he asked, leaning forward.

"If you can give me some background on this case off-the-record now, we'll be ready with a story that ensures you get the credit you deserve when you're ready to go public. We want to do right by you, Sheriff."

"I see," he said with a dry laugh. "And the *Louisville Post* gets an exclusive scoop, of course."

Fish smiled. "I can see we understand each other, sir," she said. "Now, what can you tell me about this crime?"

# 27

**BACK IN** his motel room, Brill was relieved to be motionless – and alone. Puking his guts out had been humiliating. Worse still, maybe the bad food had been intentional. He'd need to be more cautious.

In the bathroom, he rinsed out his mouth and brushed his teeth. When he lifted the toilet lid to take care of some business, Henry spoke to him.

"A killer in Hollywood. A copycat in Kentucky," his deep voice said.

Henry usually spoke when Brill opened something – a drawer, a door, even a can of beer. But the toilet seat was a first.

What did Henry mean this time?

His advice was usually puzzling, at first anyway. But Henry had helped him solve a case more than once. That's why Brill couldn't tell anyone about Henry. He didn't want to share the credit.

Brill weighed Henry's words again: A killer in Hollywood.

*Who was a killer in Hollywood?* The answer came like a lightning bolt.

*Charles Manson.*

Yes, it all made sense now. Manson was a half-assed musician who had killed a house full of show-biz types in revenge for not making a record of his music.

The two hippies he was chasing weren't hit men. They were Manson copycats.

# 28

**WE'D BEEN** on this bus ride from hell for nearly twelve hours when we passed a sign that said Welcome to Michigan. Just being cooped up that long was bad enough. Reading the paperback copy of *Doors of Perception* I'd brought didn't help. Huxley's book about mescaline was a reminder of our biggest hassle.

We'd smoked the last of our weed three stops back.

Anybody who tells you reefer's not addictive has probably never quit smoking it. I mean, it's not like going off smack cold turkey, okay? But if you've ever been around someone jonesing for a cigarette or a cup of coffee and being a total dick, then you'll have an idea of how Peanut and I felt.

"Jesus, we're only at the Michigan border? How much longer until we get to Detroit?" Peanut whispered to me, then sniffled.

"What am I, the goddam conductor?" I whispered back. We were getting really good at low decibel bickering. "And blow your nose, goddamit. Your sniffling is driving me crazy. It's like listening to nose farts."

"What about you?" Peanut snapped. "Checking out your hair in the window like a thousand times a day. You think that doesn't get old?"

As the bus pulled into a rest area, I took a deep breath. "Look, maybe we should get off and grab something to eat." I said, realizing it was the lack of cannabis talking.

While we waited for the passengers in front of us to file off the bus, I looked out the window. Could the Paducah cops or the feds arrest us in Canada? I wasn't sure. But of all the places we could go, Canada seemed our best bet. Maybe Chester was on to something. After all, draft dodgers and deserters were safe there. I kept these doubts to myself, though. Peanut was already shaky about the plan.

A raw wind cut through my jacket like a blade as we stepped off the bus. I tightened my collar and walked toward a line of vending machines under a shelter with Peanut behind me.

The candy machine didn't have any Crunch Bars and Peanut was pissed at having to settle for a Chunky. So I shouldn't have been surprised by what he said.

"I think this whole draft-dodging thing is crazy, man," Peanut grumbled, taking the chocolate bar out of the machine.

I looked around to make sure we were alone, then said, "What the hell's your problem, man?"

"Well, we're supposed to pretend we're draft dodgers so somebody will help us get across the border – but what if they bust us for draft dodging when we try to get to Canada?"

"Jesus, Peanut. For someone whose head is too big for his body, it's a shame yours is mostly bone," I said. "How can they bust us for draft dodging if we're not being drafted?"

Peanut ripped the foil off the Chunky and took a bite. "I don't know – anyway it's freezing up here," he mumbled as he chewed. "I want to go back to Miami, man. We can lay low until all this blows over."

"This is not going to blow over, goddamit," I said,

trying not to scream. "I've had time to think this through, man. We can't go back."

"Why not?"

"Half the goddam town of Paducah saw us in Vardon's Mustang the day he was killed. The cops will track that car back to Donny in Miami and find out who we are. The heat does not give up on murder cases, man. If we go back to Miami, they'll hunt us down," I said.

Peanut took another bite and shrugged. "Maybe."

"Hey, if that's not bad enough, it's only a matter of time before the feds catch up with Alvin. After that, they'll find out about the hundred you broke in the motel bar and the feds will come looking for us too."

"You think they'd come after us for passing one fake bill?"

"I don't know. But I'm not taking a chance on spreading more bad money," I said, getting an idea. "Give me the other four Bennies Alvin gave you."

"What for?"

"C'mon, I'll show you," I said, walking behind the building, out of sight of the other passengers. Then I took out my five fake hundreds, struck a spark with my lighter and set them on fire. I held them until my fingers were nearly singed before letting them drop.

"You're out of your goddam mind, man!" Peanut said, watching the bills turn to ashes on the concrete.

"Now give me yours."

"No way."

"Look, man. We've got the heat after us for Vardon's murder. Even if they caught us and we managed to somehow get out of it, we'd *still* get charged with counterfeiting as long as we have those bills on us."

"But we might need that bread for an emergency or something."

"Don't be stupid, Maxwell," I said, using his given name. I wanted him to know this was serious. "That money is a ticket to jail."

Peanut stared hard at me. I could see him trying to decide. He pulled out his wallet and held out the bills. "I hope like hell we don't regret this, Cruiser," he said and sighed. "'Cause pretty soon, all we'll have left is pocket lint."

# 29

**APPROACHING THE** suburbs of Indianapolis in the Fairmont, Fish took another bite of Slim Jim and gulped down some cold coffee. The snacks she'd grabbed three hours ago while filling up the tank near the sheriff's office would have to be her lunch.

Although her targets had left Paducah by bus at eleven last night, Erna could still beat them to Detroit if she stayed on the main highways without breaks for food. Unlike the bus, she didn't have to stop in every clodhopper *dorf* along the way.

The sheriff had told her everything about their two prime suspects: their names, what they looked like and every place they'd been seen around Paducah.

He'd also complained bitterly that an FBI agent from Louisville had taken over the case. The fed had killed any news stories and limited the sheriff's investigation to McCracken County.

While the sheriff believed the two hippies called Cruiser and Peanut were the hitmen, the FBI agent did not. Whatever Hoover's bozo was up to, however, the sheriff had no idea. "My hands are tied – and if the shit hits the fan on this case, I damned well want the press to know that," he'd said.

The sheriff thought taking the bus was a brilliant escape scheme. The killers had an opportunity to flee from any of the small towns along the route to Detroit. But Erna knew Cruiser and Peanut were not the killers.

They were the two guys she'd spotted in the Mustang at Vardon's cabin – a couple of hippie chumps who had stumbled onto a murder scene while delivering a car for cash. Erna had figured that out when Sheri Jean said the hippies expected a thousand dollars for returning the Mustang.

The hippies had planned to leave Paducah on the bus all along. Nothing else made sense.

Luckily for her, these two dopes were the perfect fall guys. Her plan when she caught up with them was brutally simple.

She'd nab the pair at gun point, take them into the woods and finish them off. Then she'd plant the Uzi on the bodies and tip off the sheriff. The scene would look like the killers had taken each other out during a dispute.

With the prime suspects identified, the sheriff's gag order would end – and she'd finally get paid.

After passing another truck, Fish yawned and reached for the bottle of bennies.

It was nearly empty.

# 30

**CARL'S SHIFT** at the Hickory Tree started at six each evening. It wasn't long after that when a chubby guy in a black suit with a six-strand combover entered the lounge. He sort of looked like Gig Young – if Gig had been having an allergic reaction to penicillin.

Although the guy didn't fit the TV image, he was still easy to make as an FBI agent. Carl had been expecting him.

The fed took the first seat at the bar and waved Carl over. The two salesmen at the other end of the counter took no notice. Their radars were only scanning for women.

"What will you have, sir?" Carl asked, not tipping his hand.

The agent slid a wallet with a badge toward him on the counter. "Jack Brill, Special Agent. FBI."

Carl nodded and waited for the fed to make his play.

"I understand you waited on a couple of hippies here last night."

"That's right."

"Your boss told us they paid with counterfeit money. A hundred-dollar bill to be exact."

"I'm not an expert on that sort of thing. The bill looked fine to me."

"You didn't think it was unusual for a pair of longhairs to be carrying that kind of money?"

"I get paid to serve drinks, sir. Not judge my customers."

The agent gave Carl a hard look. "Was Sheri Jean Jenkins in here last night?"

"Yes, sir."

"What was her relationship with these hippies?"

"Sheri Jean was playing pool with some other customers. She seemed to know the hippies and talked to them for a couple of minutes before she left."

"That's all?"

"That's all I saw."

The agent's face tightened as he leaned closer to the bartender. "Let me tell you something, Carl. I've been with the FBI eleven years. I've chased murderers, kidnappers, arsonists, and bunko artists," he said. "This pair is the worst I've run across," he growled. "I'll come down hard on anyone who withholds evidence. You understand me?"

"I understand, sir," Carl said calmly.

Carl exhaled with relief when the fed left the bar. He was afraid of Agent Jack Brill. But Alvin Jenkins had paid him a visit earlier today. And he feared Alvin even more.

31

**PANCHO WAS** looking pretty skinny as we followed Chester out of the bus station. The only thing left inside my travel bag were extra underwear and my copies of *Doors of Perception* and *Stranger in a Strange Land*.

Peanut and I had put on all the other threads we'd brought on the trip in the men's room after getting off the bus. With the sun setting, Detroit was like the inside of a freezer – and my *huevos* were already turning into ice cubes.

On the sidewalk, Chester gave us directions to Plum Street, then shook our hands. "Like I said, you'll find other young folk down there who might be able to help you," he said. "I don't envy you boys. But I think you're doing the right thing, trying to stay out of that useless war. Good luck to you."

After Chester walked away, Peanut said, "I feel like a shitheel, man."

"Yeah, me too," I said. "But don't forget. It's not like we killed those guys or cheated anybody, man. We're just trying to survive." The excuse didn't make me feel much better, though.

By the time we reached Plum Street, I was shivering and my cheeks were numb – both face and butt. Thankfully, just as Chester had predicted, finding somebody to help us across the border didn't take long.

After flashing the peace sign and starting up conversations with a few freaks on Plum, they gave us directions to a head shop down the street. Working at the store was a guy named Kurt who was part of a student group that helped resisters get into Canada.

"I'll take you guys across," Kurt told us. "But not if you're holding, okay?"

"We're clean, man," I said.

"Yeah. So clean it hurts," Peanut added.

"I get off work at nine. You guys can wait in the storeroom," Kurt said, leading us through a door at the back of the shop. "It's probably better if you stay out of sight."

# 32

**PARKED WITHIN** sight of the bus terminal doorway, Fish downed her last benny.

Despite the thoughts darting like jackrabbits through her brain, she was fighting to stay awake. This contract was turning into the shittiest of her career. But it had one thing in common with all the others.

Most of the time she spent on a hit was waiting.

She operated like a chameleon, an ambush predator who changed its skin to blend with the surroundings until the moment came to strike its unsuspecting prey.

Today, her camouflage was as a streetwalker – a look she managed with a beehive wig, heavy mascara, high heel pumps with fishnet stockings and a mini-skirt peeking under a leather bomber jacket.

Normally, Erna wouldn't pose as a criminal during a job. That was begging for attention from the cops.

But she couldn't come up with anything better. She was too old to pass as one of the teeny boppers who hung out in downtown Detroit. A thirty-something hooker, however, wouldn't seem out of place in this seedy section of the city.

Fish had considered posing as a bag lady. But someone who looked homeless getting in and out of a new car was sure to draw unwanted attention.

Her vision started to blur again. The headache would come next. It was the bennies. You couldn't cheat your body out of sleep forever.

Fish checked her watch. With any luck, the bus from Paducah would be on schedule and arrive soon.

Rubbing her temples and straining to focus, Erna spotted a pair of hippies leaving the bus station. One was tall and good looking, the other one short with a bruise on his head. This had to be Cruiser and Peanut.

Fish got out of the car and began tailing them. She was almost certain where they were headed. The hippies in Detroit hung out on Plum Street.

Her targets stopped and talked to several other longhairs along Plum. One of them led Cruiser and Peanut across the street into a drug paraphernalia store. The moment she'd been waiting for had arrived.

With her targets off the street, Fish could pull out her snub nose and herd them back to her car with the .38 concealed in her coat. She'd make the little one drive while keeping the gun on both of them from the back seat. Once they were in the countryside, she'd finish the job.

As Fish began to cross the street, a Corvette pulled up, cutting her off.

Rolling down the window, the driver called out. "Hey, sugar. You doing business?"

"Get lost," she said without looking at the driver.

As Fish began to walk behind the car, the john backed up the Vette, blocking her path.

When she moved in the opposite direction, the driver pulled forward. "I'm just looking for a blow job, babe," he said.

On edge from the pills, Erna snapped.

Pulling the snub nose from her coat pocket, she pointed the gun through the window and cocked the hammer. "You want a blow job, asshole? How about I blow your brains into the street?"

Peeling rubber, the Corvette sped away.

Fish watched the car leave, then put the revolver back in her pocket.

As she began to cross the street, Fish heard a horn blare and turned toward the sound.

Erna Herring's last sight was the grill of a Mack truck hurtling toward her.

**33**

**THE STOREROOM** in the head shop was lit by a naked bulb in the ceiling. Stacked at random against the walls were boxes of bongs, roach clips, rolling papers, dayglo posters, UV lights and t-shirts.

"Check this out, Cruiser," Peanut said as he found a box of *Zap* comics. "I haven't read this *Fritz the Cat* yet."

"Knock yourself out, man," I said, brushing the dust off a box of Zig-Zag papers and sitting down. I was glad we were out of the cold. But we were still not out of trouble.

Since we'd stumbled onto the bodies at Vardon's house twenty-four hours ago, we'd been on the run, constantly looking over our shoulders for the law. And for what? I'd wanted to change my life somehow. So I quit my job and went on this trip. Now I was sitting in the frozen bowels of Detroit, feeling nostalgic for the smell of monkey shit.

My pity party was interrupted by a siren coming from the street.

Peanut jumped to his feet. "We need to book, Cruiser! The heat is on to us."

I was grabbing for Pancho when Kurt opened the door.

"A hooker just got hit by a truck out front. Stay cool, guys," Kurt said, then left.

"That's a relief," I said, sitting down again.

"She could be dead, Cruiser," Peanut said, settling back onto the boxes.

"What? You're my fucking Jiminy Cricket now?" I said

– then suddenly felt like shit. "Sorry, man. You're right."

Looking for a distraction, I reached into Pancho and pulled out my copy of *Stranger*.

Reading didn't help. Instead of escaping into the story, my mind kept drifting back to feeling-sorry-for-Cruiser land.

After an endless wait, Kurt led us to his car. We were finally headed for Canada.

I was expecting a ten-foot wall topped with barbed wire and guard towers with machine guns. But the border between the U.S. and Canada looked like a freeway toll station.

"Are you sure it's this easy, man?" I asked Kurt.

"Don't sweat it. We do this all the time," Kurt assured us.

"I thought they'd be checking Selective Service cards and stuff, looking for draft dodge—I mean resisters," Peanut said.

Kurt laughed softly. "No, man. The Canadians aren't allowed to do that anymore," he said. "But there's just one thing. Whatever they ask about your background, tell the truth, okay? It's a federal offense if they catch you in a lie."

In spite of everything Kurt had said, my mouth was still dry as we pulled up to the only booth still open. It was after eleven and the guard inside looked cold and bored.

Kurt rolled down the window. "Good evening," he said politely.

The guard shined his flashlight into the car, scanning our faces. "Place of birth?" he asked.

"Lansing, Michigan," Kurt said.

"Waycross, Georgia," Peanut answered.

I swallowed hard. "Havana, Cuba," I croaked.

The guard rolled his eyes and pointed to a parking space next to a building marked Customs & Immigration. "Pull over there," he said.

For the first time, Kurt looked a little shook. "I had no idea you were a Cuban. You sure don't look like one."

Peanut, who had grown up in Miami's casserole of cultures, set him straight. "Man, you haven't seen a lot of Cubans, have you? They come in every color."

Kurt shrugged. "I think it should be okay, though. You're an American citizen, right?" he said, pulling into the parking space.

"Technically, I'm a refugee," I said. "I have a green card – but I'm not actually a citizen."

Kurt closed his eyes and rubbed the bridge of his nose. "Okay," he said slowly. "We'll see how this goes."

Those were not the words I wanted to hear. I'd felt bad about letting Kurt think we were draft dodgers. But now I felt even worse. This whole goddam idea might get us all into some deep shit.

Peanut touched my shoulder from the back seat. "I think that guard is the only one here," he said nodding toward the cop in the booth who was now on the phone. "We can make a run for it."

"Guys," Kurt said nervously, "I wouldn't do that." He looked pale and scared, his earlier confidence gone.

Before I could decide, the door on the Customs & Immigration building opened and the guard waved us inside.

A gray-haired cop with three chevrons on his sleeve sat behind a high counter. He motioned for us to step forward. My heart began to thump when I noticed a camera on the wall. We lined up, staring at our shoes, like three criminals before a judge.

"All right then. May I see some identification, please."

Peanut and Kurt handed the guy their IDs. Trying to keep my hands from shaking, I held out my green card which I'd gotten shortly after we arrived in Miami from Havana.

"You're the gentleman born in Cuba, I see," he said to me, looking at my green card. "Do you have any identification that's more recent?" The picture on the card was taken when I was eleven.

"Sure," I said, struggling to sound calm as I gave him my Florida Driver's License.

A trickle of sweat ran down my back as the guard studied our cards, holding each one up to the light at one point. Then he opened a three-ring binder and checked our names against some kind of list.

Peanut and I looked at each other. I knew we were both silently asking the same question. Would the cops already have some kind of bulletin out on us? As we stood there, I imagined us being taken away in handcuffs... I saw a jail cell door clanging shut... I saw an old man with gray hair in a striped uniform looking at a tiny patch of sky through a barred window.

The guard looked up and held out our IDs. "Welcome to Canada," he said curtly.

"Do you have a restroom?" I asked, about to piss my pants.

# 34

**KURT STOPPED** his car in front of the Rose City Coffee Shop. "Your contact works here. Her name is Sunshine," he told us, then gestured for us to get out.

We smiled and gave Kurt the peace sign as he drove away. Kurt stared straight ahead.

"I bet he was glad to get rid of us," Peanut said. "Kurt told us he never had any hassles getting guys across before - until *you* came along."

"Shut up," I said, walking toward the coffee shop door. I felt crappy about what happened with Kurt but arguing with Peanut was getting old. I thought he'd be grateful we were finally in Canada and out of danger. Instead, he was giving me this crappy vibe. Okay, maybe being tired, wired and jonesing for weed wasn't making Zen monks out of either of us.

Stepping inside, I was surprised to see the coffee shop still busy. A clock on the wall said it was quarter after eleven. Most of the people in the place were our age, a lot of them hunched over books.

"Maybe it's exam week," I said, dropping Pancho into a booth and sliding next to it.

"I wouldn't know," Peanut said, sitting down across from me, "I didn't spend two whole semesters at Miami Dade Junior College."

"Listen, Peanut," I said, getting pissed, "I've had about enough of—"

Before I could finish, our waitress appeared. "Hi," she said with a gentle smile. "You guys need menus?" She smelled like fresh jelly donuts.

My pissy mood vanished. Although Kurt's description did not do her justice, I knew right away this was our contact. "You must be Sunshine," I said, beaming. She had a face like a saint on a church statue and blonde hair that hung all the way to her waist. I've always had a weakness for women with long hair.

"Yeah," she said, not surprised I knew her name. She probably got hit on more often than a crosswalk button on Flagler Street. "What can I get you?"

"Kurt sent us," I said softly. "He said to tell you we needed tickets for the railroad."

"Yeah, railroad tickets," Peanut whispered, oogling Sunshine like a schnauzer in a butcher shop. The little shit was finally seeing eye-to-eye with me on something. We both instantly had the hots for Sunshine.

Sunshine nodded serenely. "We close at midnight. Meantime, I'll get you guys some coffee – it's on the house," she said and walked back to the kitchen.

Peanut picked up the table's chrome napkin dispenser, held it near his brow, and looked at his reflection. "The bump doesn't look so bad. What do you think?"

The swelling was gone, replaced by nasty yellow and purple blotches. "I think you're wasting your time, man. Your forehead could be as smooth as a baby's ass and Sunshine would still think you're dog-butt ugly."

Sunshine came back with two cups of coffee. "Here you go," she said, putting the mugs down in front of us. Then, on the sly, she took a car key from her apron and slid it on the table. "My VW bus is in the parking lot out back," she said softly. "When we start closing, let your-selves in and wait for me."

I watched Sunshine walk away, awash in impure thoughts – until Peanut ruined my fantasy.

"Sunshine's a babe, man. But I'm ready to go back to Miami," Peanut said.

I rolled my eyes. "Peanut, when will you get it through your thick skull? The heat will find us there."

"Yeah? Well, I've been thinking," Peanut said, tapping his temple. "If the heat was really after us, why didn't the guard at the border have our names on that list?"

"I see," I said, rubbing my forehead. "So the only way you'll be convinced the cops are looking for us is when they haul us off to jail. That's absolutely brilliant."

"I think you're being paranoid."

"Hey, if you want to go back to Miami – go," I said pulling out my wallet. "I've got seven bucks left. How much have you got?"

Peanut checked his wallet. "Eleven."

"My guess is that eighteen bucks will buy you a bus ticket to somewhere in Ohio. You can hitch the rest of the way. It might get a little cold – and you might get the shit kicked out of you by some rednecks. But, what the hell? You'll be back home," I said, then added. "By the way, after you get back to Miami, send me a postcard – if your cellmate Leroy lets you take your mouth off his *pinga* long enough to lick a stamp."

Peanut looked pissed but clammed up. When the clock reached midnight, he picked up his bag and said, "Time to go."

Walking behind the building, we reached the parking lot. "Wow. Can you believe that?" I said to Peanut, spotting

Sunshine's microbus. Someone had replaced the usual big VW logo on the front with a peace sign. "In Miami, that would be like painting 'bust me' on your ride."

"No shit. Maybe the heat's not so bad up here because it's so goddam cold," Peanut said, then gave me a Bugs Bunny wink.

"Oooh, Peanut. Write that one down and send it to Richard Pryor. I'm sure he'll open his act with it next time he's in Canada."

We got in the microbus and before long, Sunshine joined us. "Welcome to peace and freedom, guys," she said, starting the engine.

As Sunshine headed down the road, we introduced ourselves and told her we were from Miami. Needless to say, we kept all the crazy shit in Paducah to ourselves.

"Where are we headed, Sunshine?" Peanut asked. As usual, he was in the back seat.

"Our commune will put you up tonight. Tomorrow, we'll tell you how to get to Toronto."

"Why Toronto?" I asked.

"We don't have the resources to help resisters much around here. Besides, it's always good to get you guys away from the border."

"How did you get into this whole resistance thing?" I asked her, noticing that we were now out of the city.

"Everybody in our commune is trying to get back to the land, you know? I work in town to bring in some cash until we can quit the system. We also believe in giving peace a chance. So we help resisters like you get out of the belly of the beast."

"Wow," I said, nodding.

Listening to Sunshine made me feel like a double

poser. Peanut and I weren't just fake draft dodgers. We were half-assed city hippies too.

# 35

**"WE'RE HERE,"** Sunshine said, turning into an unpaved drive. The mailbox by the road had Celestial Fields painted in psychedelic lettering above the house number.

In the headlights I saw an old farmhouse and a barn surrounded by a weird collection of structures. As we got closer, I could make out a geodesic dome, a hodge-podge of shacks made from lumber scraps and a school bus without wheels.

"How many of you live here?" Peanut asked.

"Hard to say for sure. People come and go. But usually it's around thirty."

After parking the microbus, Sunshine led us into the farmhouse. About a dozen people were sitting in a circle on the floor of the living room, passing a pipe. The only light in the room came from a pile of wood burning in the fireplace.

"Kurt dropped off another pair," Sunshine announced as we walked in.

"Far out," one of the guys on the floor said, holding out the pipe. "You guys into some kief?"

Peanut's eyes lit up. "For sure, man," he said sitting down on the floor.

"Toke up," Sunshine said, gesturing toward the group. "I'll be back in a minute."

As the pipe went around, I noticed that Peanut and I were the only guys without full beards. Peanut's Fu Manchu and my goat looked slick and plastic in comparison. The women looked like less stunning versions of Sunshine—no makeup, straight hair and granny dresses.

The guy beside me passed the pipe and I took a hit of kief, my first THC infusion in several days. By the time I exhaled, I was half baked.

After the pipe had been around a couple of times, Sunshine walked in from the kitchen carrying an oil lantern and said, "You guys are probably wiped out. C'mon, I'll show you where to crash."

We followed Sunshine into the kitchen. "Is that where you guys cook?" Peanut asked, walking past an iron stove that looked like a prop from a cowboy movie. A large bucket of water was simmering on its top. "You could have a tank of cooking gas put in and save a lot of work."

"Burning wood is more work, for sure," Sunshine said. "But wood is renewable. Cooking gas isn't."

"Don't you use kerosene in that lamp?" Peanut asked, pointing at Sunshine's lantern like he'd caught her cheating at something.

"We use lampante olive oil," Sunshine answered.

"Far out," I said. "You guys are for real."

Sunshine led us out the side door to the bus without wheels I'd noticed driving in. "Welcome to the Celestial Fields hotel," she said, opening the door. "We always keep this place open for resisters."

She raised the lantern so we could look around. All the seats were gone, replaced by pieces of mismatched carpeting. Sheets hung over most of the windows. At the back of the bus was a small potbellied stove. Beside it, a stack of wood.

"I'll get a fire started. You guys pick out a sleeping bag," she said, nodding toward a pile of them rolled up near the door.

"This commune reminds me of how some of my kin in Georgia live," Peanut said, unrolling a green army surplus sleeping bag. "They ain't got two nickels to rub together, as my mom likes to say."

"We share whatever we have equally," Sunshine said, opening the stove door and loading it with wood. "We're trying to live the way God intended."

"I guess that takes some sacrifices," I said, handing Sunshine more wood.

"I think what you did is much harder," she said, our eyes meeting. "You left everything you knew to follow your convictions. That took courage *and* sacrifice."

Man, did *that* make me feel slimy. "Really, it isn't that big of a deal."

Sunshine sat down beside me. "You don't have to be modest. I can only imagine what you're going through," she said, putting her hand on my arm.

"I'm more interested in how this commune got started," I said, eager to change the subject. "Are you one of the originals?"

Sunshine seemed proud that I asked. For the next fifteen minutes, I got the history of the commune going back to the local rock band, who along with their groupies, had pooled their money to buy the property. By the time Sunshine was done, we were leaning close to each other on the floor. Peanut was in his sleeping bag and snoring.

"Look, I know it's late, but is there any chance to get a bath?" I asked softly. "We've been on the road for days."

Sunshine smiled. "Actually, I was about to take a bath myself," she said. "I've got water heating in the kitchen. We can share it and help the planet."

"I'd love that," I whispered. "But I'm pretty sure someone around here is going to be upset about that invitation. You're way too lovely not to have a boyfriend."

"That won't be a problem, Cruiser. I'm in an open relationship."

Quietly, we slipped out of the bus and went back to the house. After picking up the bucket of water Sunshine was heating on the stove, we carried it to the bathroom. Next to a clawfoot tub, we got out of our clothes. Then we slowly gave each other a sponge bath. By the time we were done, Sunshine and I were like two pieces of hot toast begging to be buttered. We made love in the tub, her damp body glistening in the soft lamp light.

Man, I came to appreciate ecology in a whole new way.

# 36

**"THIS IS** the best place to catch a ride," Sunshine said after pulling the VW to the shoulder of the divided highway. "Drivers will have plenty of room to pick you up here. I really wish I could take you all the way to Toronto."

Around us as far as I could see was flat farmland covered with a dusting of snow. It reminded me of frosted shredded wheat. "I understand," I said, getting Pancho out of the microbus. "You're the bread winner for the commune."

Peanut said nothing, very loudly, as he stepped out of the sliding door behind me with his bag.

With a wave and a peace sign, Sunshine drove away.

I looked west for any traffic heading our way. There wasn't much. There was plenty of cold wind, though.

"It sucks that Sunshine couldn't drive us to Toronto," Peanut said, kicking a rock along the shoulder.

"Hey, man. Be grateful they gave us some warm clothes."

At the commune, Sunshine had offered us some leftover winter gear from a cardboard box. Along with a green fatigue jacket and some gloves, I'd grabbed a black wool hat that looked like something left behind by a Cossack. When it was Peanut's turn at the box, the only hat left was a hunter's cap with earflaps that made him look like Elmer Fudd.

"Did Sunshine say how long the drive is to Toronto?" Peanut asked, buttoning up a pea coat three sizes too big.

"About four hours."

"If someone doesn't pick us up, we could freeze to death out here, man."

"Then stick out your thumb and smile, *pendejo*," I said. "And put your hat on. It'll keep you warmer."

"No fucking way, man. I'd rather die."

For the next couple of hours, we stood by the side of the highway, flashing our thumbs at every vehicle going by. There was only one good thing about the cold. Peanut's bruise started to fade like he'd been using an icepack.

With my teeth chattering, I said, "Let's walk, man. We'll stay warmer."

When Peanut put on his hat, I didn't give him any shit about it. There wasn't much traffic and we were starting to get desperate.

"Would you live in a commune?" Peanut asked as we started down the highway.

"I never really thought about it."

"I wouldn't," Peanut said, shaking his head. "My mom left Georgia to get away from that kind of shit. It sucks to be dirt poor, man. There's nothing holy about it."

"There were a lot of people in Cuba who lived like that. My uncle always said the revolution was about helping them out. My dad didn't agree with him, though," I said. "I'm still not sure which one is right. But it seems like there are some freaks trying to start a revolution so we can all become like the poor people in Cuba."

"That's some heavy shit, man."

We stood there for a moment, not sure what to say. We'd stumbled onto hippie heresy.

"We should keep walking," I said.

About a quarter mile later, I saw a green semi with an open bed trailer in the distance and stuck out my thumb.

"Man, I'll even ride in the back of that thing," I said, pointing to the open bed of the truck to give the driver the idea. Peanut picked up on it and started pointing too.

"He's stopping, Cruiser!" Peanut screamed. "He's stopping!"

The truck was over a hundred yards down the road before it rolled to a stop. We broke into a run like the guy being chased by cannibals in *The Naked Prey*.

Always a better athlete, the little shit got to the truck first.

"What's wrong with the truck, eh?" the driver asked when Peanut opened the passenger door.

Totally clueless about the driver's question, we both climbed inside the cab with our bags. Then it hit me. The driver thought we were signaling about a problem with his truck. I decided it was best to play dumb. "Thanks for picking us up!"

"You're a lifesaver, man," Peanut added. "We were about to turn into popsicles out there."

Taking pity on us, the driver's face changed from chafed to chummy. "How far you two going?"

"Toronto," I said.

"I can get you there," the driver said. "I'm deadheading to Ottawa."

"Far out," Peanut said, taking off the Elmer Fudd hat.

"You two from the States?" the driver asked as he double clutched and steered back onto the highway.

"Yeah," I said. Although it wasn't completely true, I'd had enough hairsplitting about my nationality for a while. Peanut didn't argue the point either.

We shared first names and learned the driver went by Ned. After that, we didn't have much more to say.

Then I noticed a military ribbon attached to the dash - a pair of red and green bars flanking a blue square. "You were a Canadian Volunteer?" I asked, remembering a book I'd read in junior high when I was into soldier stuff.

Ned nodded. "I did my bit in the war."

"What was that like?" Peanut asked.

For the next hour, Ned told us about landing at Juno Beach on D-Day and his unit's march through France. Most of it wasn't battle stuff. He told us about the stupid shit his buddies did to mess with each other and the different kinds of crops they grew in France. Ned was raised on a farm in Alberta.

Ned lit a cigarette and seemed ready to talk about something else. "You're not the first young guys with long hair I've seen hitching out of Windsor," he said, his eyes on the road. "I've got a fair idea why."

My mouth turned dry. This guy thought we were real draft dodgers. I wondered if he'd make us get out. I didn't expect what Ned said next.

"The world's changed a lot since I was your age," he said. "I'm not sure I'd volunteer for a war in Vietnam."

"Thanks for going to war back then, man," Peanut said. "We might be talking in Nazi right now if you hadn't."

Ned smiled and jerked his thumb behind him. "There's a thermos with some hot buttered rum behind the seat, Peanut. Break that out and let's have a round."

By the time we hit the outskirts of Toronto, the sun was beginning to set. The rum was gone and we'd sung songs and told jokes like a bunch of kids on a sleepover.

Ned pulled the rig onto the shoulder and stopped. "I can't take you any closer to the city without setting myself back an hour," he said, then pointed to some buildings beyond an open field. "About a quarter mile that way, you'll find a subway stop that will take you into town."

Ned's mention of the subway worried me. "Does the subway take American money? That's all we've got."

Ned reached into his pocket. "The fare into the city is thirty cents," he said passing Peanut a fistful of coins. "That should be enough to get both of you there."

I wanted to hug the guy but held out my palm instead. "Thank you, Ned."

He shook both our hands and said, "You boys take care, eh?"

We watched Ned's rig pull away until it was out of sight.

Then we started hoofing it across the frozen field.

# 37

**THE SKYLINE** of Detroit appeared around a bend of I-75, a forlorn strip of gray towers shrouded in smog. Brill weaved through the endless stream of semis, looking for an exit with a motel sign.

Tracking Cruiser and Peanut to Detroit had not been hard.

The bus company gave him the name and phone number of the driver on the night the pair left Paducah. Over the phone, the driver recalled the two hippies aboard his bus. "They made friends with an old Colored boy with some kinda musical instrument," the driver told him. "The beatniks and the Colored left the station together in Detroit."

Before Brill had departed for Detroit, the sheriff made his case for a manhunt again. "You sure about holding off on an all-points bulletin?"

"What good would it do?" Brill told the sheriff. "An APB with nothing more to go on than 'a pair of hippies' fits a hundred-thousand creeps across the country. I don't want these scumbags to see me coming."

Brill hadn't told the sheriff the pair were Manson copycats. He wanted to collar them first. That way, no one could steal his glory.

As darkness fell, Brill found a motel just off the interstate near downtown. The room would be his base for following their trail. The easy part was over. Tracking the pair down within Detroit would take some work.

He'd start fresh on that in the morning. Settling in, he ordered a pizza and got back to his Nick Carter novel.

Around eleven, Brill began his nightly ritual. As he opened the bottle of Jack Daniels, Henry spoke.

"*Razzmatazz*," the sonorous voice said.

Brill poured a tot into one of the motel's tumblers and sat down. Taking a sip of bourbon, Brill let the word marinate in his brain. *Razzmatazz*. The word sounded musical – and it rhymed with jazz. Could that mean something for this case?

Brill finished his drink without a clue. Stumped and tired, he got the copy of *True Detective* from his valise and completed the final stage of his routine, then turned in for the night.

Just after midnight, Brill awoke with a start.

*Razzmatazz... Jazz. ...Musical instrument.*

The old guy on the bus had been carrying a musical instrument. Brill rose and turned on the light, then opened the Yellow Pages beside the room's telephone. The list he wanted was on page 143: *Jazz Clubs*. There were four within walking distance of the bus station.

After hurriedly getting dressed, Brill peeled rubber out of the motel parking lot. Most jazz clubs were just hitting their stride at midnight.

The first two clubs he tried were dry holes. The managers had not hired any new acts or sidemen over the last few days.

At the third club, Brill hit a gusher. The manager pointed out Chester Strachan on the stage, a replacement trumpet player for their house band.

"Is Chester in some kind of trouble?" the manager asked Brill.

"I just have some questions for him."

When the Pope Pearson Quintet took a break, the manager spoke quietly to Chester. A minute later, the musician stood before Brill in the manager's office.

"I'm Special Agent Jack Brill of the FBI," the fed said, flashing his credentials.

"The manager told me who you are," Chester said stiffly. "What do you want with me?"

"You arrived in Detroit by bus two days ago, is that right?"

Chester nodded. "I did."

"Did you make any friends on the trip?"

"There are very few people in this world I call friends. None of them was on that bus."

"Mr. Strachan, the bus driver reported you made friends with a pair of hippies during the trip. Do you recall that?"

"I may have said a few words. I wouldn't call it making friends."

"Did you get their names?" Brill asked then added. "Before you answer, you should know that lying to an FBI officer can be prosecuted for perjury."

Chester cleared his throat. "Cruiser and Peanut," he said grudgingly.

"Are those their real names?"

"How would I know?"

"You were seen leaving the bus station with these two. Where did they go?"

Chester's eyes narrowed. "I told those boys about the neighborhood around Plum Street where they could find other people like them. That was the last time I saw them. That's not a crime for me or for them, is it?" he asked, fuming.

"What do you mean, 'other people like them'?"

"Folks who can see this country's gone wrong. Young people who think we've got no business being in this war – and nobody's listening to them. That's why there's so many young men looking to get across that river."

The bile rose in Brill's throat. "I can't imagine your kind feels any shame about helping draft dodgers," he said with a sneer.

"Oh. I feel ashamed, all right. But it ain't about helping those boys," Chester said, then held up his left hand. "I feel ashamed I lost these fingers at Bastogne so peckerwoods like you would put people in jail for doing what they think is right."

"You can go," Brill said, waving Chester away like a fly. His mind was locked on collaring these perps.

This Cruiser and Peanut pair weren't just wanton killers and counterfeiters. They were traitors as well.

# 38

**THE FIELD** we were about to cross was at the edge of Toronto's suburbs. Behind us was nothing but wall-to-wall farmland. Ahead of us, the field ended at the ass end of a strip mall, a row of low buildings with truck bays and dumpsters. Beyond those buildings – I hoped – was the subway that would take us downtown.

I could not wait to get my feet back on pavement again.

About halfway across the frozen field, Peanut said, "I'm hungry."

Neither of us had eaten since Sunshine had dished us up some oatmeal for breakfast – unless you counted Ned's rum as nourishment.

"I'm hungry too," I said. "But we're not going to starve to death just yet."

Picking up the pace, Peanut said, "I have a great-uncle back in Georgia who ate a spider. Bit him in the mouth and damn near killed him."

"Why in the hell did he eat a spider?"

"He saw it on the floor and thought it was a raisin," Peanut said, shaking his head. "Uncle Roger was a cheap motherfucker. He needed glasses but wouldn't spend the money."

After I stopped laughing, I said, "I'm not hungry enough to eat food off the floor yet."

Peanut rubbed his stomach. "I'm getting close, man."

Leaving the field, we cut through the parking lot between

two buildings and caught sight of the subway entrance on the other side the street.

My eyes lit up. Civilization at last.

Peanut took off the Elmer Fudd hat and stuffed it in his bag.

We entered the subway stop, relishing the warmth. After paying for our tickets, we went down a stairway to the train line. Looking at the line map, Peanut pointed to a stop called Bloor-Yonge. "This is it, right?" he asked.

I nodded. "That's what Sunshine said, for sure."

What we'd find there, I wasn't so sure about.

## 39

**THE PASSENGERS** on the subway were your typical, plastic, office-creature commuters heading home on a sleek silver train.

Walking out of the subway terminal at Bloor and Yonge was like stepping onto another planet.

As far as you could see, the wide sidewalks were flowing rivers of long-hair, bell bottoms, mini-skirts, biker vests, go-go boots and granny dresses. Nestled against the sidewalks, stores painted in psychedelic colors sold coffee, books, baked goods, records, paintings, posters and drug paraphernalia.

Compared to this, the small and patchy head hangouts in Miami were like a half-dozen rowboats next to the Queen Mary.

"Far out," Peanut said, eyes swirling.

Walking along the street, dazzled by the scene, I'd almost forgotten how hungry I was.

Almost.

Passing a coffee shop, I spotted a small sign on the door that read: U.S. Dollars Accepted. Nudging Peanut, I said, "You got enough money left for a couple of coffees?"

"Why do we have to use *my* money?" he grumbled, reaching for his wallet.

At a corner booth in the cafe, we sat down with our coffees.

Peanut grabbed the tin cup with the cream and had it practically drained before I said, "Hey, man. Leave some for me."

After we both added three packs of sugar to our coffees, we clinked cups.

That first sip was the best drink I've ever tasted.

Peanut wiped the coffee from his chin, then smiled and held out his palm. "Give me five, Cruiser. We made it, man!"

I smiled back and slapped his hand.

Peanut leaned toward me, keeping his voice down. "I don't think the heat will find us here, man. With all these freaks around, we blend right in."

Peanut was right. After running for days, we could finally breathe easy about the law. But we had a whole new set of hassles.

We were nearly broke, in a strange country with no friends, and without a place to stay. But that wasn't all.

Was this where we'd spend the rest of our lives? Peanut seemed to be on the same wavelength.

"My mom's gonna miss me," Peanut said, staring into his coffee cup.

"My dad won't give a shit that I'm gone – and that's fine with me," I said, taking the last swig in my cup. "Drink up. We need to find a place to crash," I said, rising from my seat.

# 40

**WE WANDERED** up Bloor, looking for a friendly face.

Before long, we ran into a guy with a frizzy blond pony-tail selling some kind of newspaper. "Harbinger?" he said, holding out a copy.

Raising my palm, I said, "Sorry, man. We're broke."

"It's just a quarter, bro," he said.

Peanut gave me a shitty look as I reached into my pocket.

"You guys from out of town?" the guy asked while I fished for some change.

"No shit, Sherlock. Did the bags give us away?" Peanut said with a sneer, patting his satchel.

I handed the guy a 25-center from the Canadian coins Ned gave us. "Don't mind my friend, man," I said. "His daddy and his uncle were the same guy."

The guy took the money and said, "Thanks for supporting the people, bro."

"Hey, man," I said. "You know anyplace we can crash?"

The guy nodded. "Rochdale, man," he said. "Keep walking down Bloor. It's a tall building with a gray statue out front. It's kind of a college but people crash there all the time."

A few blocks later, we found the place.

"This must be Rochdale," I said as we walked up to a raw concrete high-rise with a gray statue by the door.

"Is that a roasted chicken?" Peanut asked, pointing at the statue.

I walked around to the front of the sculpture. "Your mind's stuck on food, man," I said. "Come look at it from this side. It's a guy sitting down with his head on his knees."

"This dude looks bummed out," Peanut said, after walking around the statue.

I hoped that wasn't an omen as we passed under an awning and opened the door.

The smell of reefer and high school lunchroom hit me as we walked inside. A lobby the size of a gym was packed with freaks. Some were sprawled over the furniture and floors. Others stood in knots or milled around. Over the buzz of their voices, I could hear someone playing a sitar. On the walls were a half-dozen life-size prints made by pressing naked bodies covered in red paint against brown paper.

"I don't think we'll have a problem finding a spot to crash," Peanut said. "But what the hell is this place?"

"The guy selling the newspaper said this was some kind of college."

"He might be right," Peanut said, pointing to the back wall of the room. "Look over there."

About twenty guys were sitting on the floor and taking notes, their eyes glued to someone lecturing. My eyes widened when I noticed their teacher.

I nudged Peanut. "I'd stay after school doing extra homework for *her*."

Under a close-cropped Afro, the teacher had Cleopatra features and caramel skin. Her eyes were so green, I could tell across the room.

Drawn by this goddess, I started toward her when Peanut grabbed my arm.

"I smell food, Cruiser. Put your *pinga* back in your

pants and let's go look for something to eat."

Following our noses, we found the entrance to a cafeteria next to a couple of elevators. I was surprised to see that, instead of old ladies with hair nets, freaks like us were serving the food.

After checking the prices and deciding we had enough Canadian change to split a burger, we got into the cafeteria line. Hippies can be a lot of great things. But efficient, we're not. The line was moving slower than a koala bear on quaaludes.

We were about six places from the trays and silver when a guy in a biker vest cut in at the head of the line.

"Who's that guy think he is?" Peanut said, then handed me his travel bag and walked toward him.

I tried to grab Peanut's arm but missed.

"Hey, man," Peanut said, tapping the biker's back.

The biker slowly turned around. His stare was something I'd only seen on vipers.

"The end of the line is back there," Peanut said, pointing his thumb behind him.

The biker's smiled – which was scarier than his stare. "Who's gonna make me go back there?"

I cringed as Peanut stared back. I knew the little shit. He was going to throw a punch.

Then, the biggest woman I'd ever seen walked up. She had rusty brown hair in a braid down her back that was thicker than a ball bat. "He's right, Gears," she said calmly to the biker. "We don't cut in line here. You know that."

This woman was *big*, man. I'm nearly six-foot and she topped me by another four or five inches. She was solid, too. In her plaid flannel shirt and bib overalls, you could picture her holding an axe on her shoulder next to a blue ox named Babe. Peanut looked like something she could carry in her pocket.

The biker rolled his eyes. "Goddamit, Cookie. You're such a downer," he said. "The burgers are better at the A&W anyway," he said, then walked out of the cafeteria.

After Peanut was beside me in line again, I whispered, "You are out of your fucking mind."

"No way I'd let some asshole pull that shit," Peanut said, shrugging his shoulders.

Once we finally got our food, Peanut and I sat down at a table, cut the burger in half with a plastic knife, and began to eat. Before we'd finished, the big woman who'd broken up Peanut's standoff walked over to us.

"I see you guys just got here," she said, pointing with her chin toward our bags. "Where are you from?"

Peanut said, "We're from Mi—"

"—from the States," I said, cutting him off. My paranoia told me there was no point in giving out too much information.

"Most Americans who show up at Rochdale didn't come here to study. I don't think you two did either. Am I right?"

I was sure Cookie thought we were draft dodgers. "Yeah, you're right," I said - which wasn't really a lie. "Thanks for stepping in on my friend's...um, conversation."

"That's what I do around here," she said. "My name's Cookie."

After we'd shared our names, Peanut said, "That biker backed down fast. Are you like the sheriff here or something?"

Cookie smiled. "Sort of. I'm the Sevak of Ashram 5-A."

"You're the what of the what?" Peanut asked

"You mind if I sit down?" Cookie asked. "This could take a while."

# 41

**WHILE PEANUT** and I picked the last scraps of hamburger off our plates, Cookie filled us in on Rochdale. Her eyes were mostly on Peanut as she spoke.

"The college started a few years back. There aren't any real classes here or any kind of grades. If you want to study something, you join a group of students who are interested in the same thing."

"No teachers?" Peanut asked.

"Not unless the students want them," Cookie answered.

"Far out," Peanut said.

"They designed this building for communal studies. Every floor is divided into units called ashrams. Each one has six or eight bedrooms with a kitchen, a lounge and a bathroom that everyone shares," Cookie said. "The students of Ashram 5-A pay me to be their Sevak – which means I keep everything in order."

"So you're, like, a maid?" Peanut asked.

"No. Everyone cleans up after themselves. I just make sure they do it," she said, flashing Peanut a smile. "I'm also a bouncer sometimes. Street people wander into our ashram once in a while."

Peanut smiled back. "So that's how you're the sheriff."

"I organize stuff too," she said, leaning closer to Peanut. "I make shopping lists and create schedules for everyone's chores."

I was picking up a vibe between these two. One I knew

quite well.

"Can you find us a place to crash tonight, Cookie?" Peanut asked.

"I can do something better," she said, putting her palm on Peanut's arm.

Peanut smiled. "I like the sound of that," he said, looking into her eyes.

I was blown away. The little shit was putting a move on Cookie.

And she was grooving on it.

"Not every ashram here has a Sevak," Cookie said, eyes glued to Peanut. "Most can't afford them. But the students in a few of the ashrams have parents with some coin. Those ashrams have a hard time finding someone who fits in here but can still do the job," she said to Peanut. "I liked how you handled yourself with Gears. Actually, he's really harmless. He wears that biker vest to scare people. But most of the freaks around here are way too timid to call him out. I think you'd make a good Sevak, Peanut," she said, eyes glowing.

"What about Cruiser?" Peanut asked, God love him.

Throwing a quick glance my way, she said, "Can you help Peanut organize?"

"Sure" I said. "What does it pay?"

Turning her gaze back to Peanut, Cookie said, "That depends on the size of the ashram. But it always includes a room and meals. From the look of you two, that alone might be a good deal."

"When can we start?" Peanut asked.

"You two can crash with me tonight," she said. "I'll check on a gig for you tomorrow."

As we headed toward the elevators, I got the feeling that tonight Peanut would be the one getting lucky.

# 42

**SITTING AT** the back of the near-empty cafe, Brill drained the last of his coffee and raised his cup, signaling the waitress for a refill.

As she topped off his mug, he looked again toward the door and then at his watch. His source had agreed to meet him here at four.

Brill had good reason to be anxious. He'd crossed more than an international border when he'd driven from Detroit to Windsor. He was crossing the line on a shitload of protocols as well.

But he wanted this pair of punks. They were the worst kind of slimeballs.

Getting an arrest warrant and an extradition order would take too long. He'd lose their trail. Going rogue was his only option. Once he tracked down Cruiser and Peanut, he'd backfill the paperwork.

Taking that shortcut had a downside, though. There was no way he could ask the local cops for help. But he was proud of his workaround. It was pure genius, he told himself.

Checking the *Windsor Star's* editorial section earlier that day, Brill had found Leonard William Perle. Every paper had a fiery conservative columnist like Perle. Brill was betting the journalist had his finger on the pulse in Windsor – and some sources willing to help him.

When the coffee shop door opened, Brill recognized

Perle from the photo on his column and waved him over.

"Mister Brill, I take it?" Perle asked after reaching the table.

Brill nodded. "Thanks for coming," he said, gesturing toward a chair.

"Do you mind if I see your credentials?" Perle asked, sitting down. "It's not every day I get a call from a U.S. FBI agent."

"Certainly," Brill said, producing his wallet.

After looking over the ID and badge, Perle said, "Why do you want to see me, Mister Brill?"

"I'm investigating some very serious crimes and I believe you can help."

"I'm always ready to assist guardians of the law."

"You get a lot of American draft dodgers in Windsor. I'd like to know how they're getting help from the locals."

"It's shameful, Mister Brill. But Windsor has become something of a port of call for cowards from your country," Perle said. "I can assure you it's simply an accident of geography. Most of the people in our city would turn away these shirkers if they could. But the leftist loonies in Ottawa—"

"I get the picture, Mister Perle," Brill said, cutting him short. "I realize most folks around here aren't helping our traitors. What I'm hoping you'll tell me is something about those who are."

"The RCMP or the CBSA can probably help you more than I can."

Brill had been expecting this. "You said it yourself, Mister Perle. A lot of government officials in Canada have been duped by the leftists. They're not very eager to help in this kind of investigation."

Perle's eyes lit up. "What our apparatchiks in government are doing is disgraceful. They've made it possible for some of our worst elements to help your draft dodgers with impunity," he said. "There's a nest of them at one of those hippie communes a few miles outside the city. They call the place Celestial Fields, can you imagine that? Living in squalor and calling it heaven."

"Can you give me directions to the commune?"

"I could but I doubt it would do you much good," Perle said. "The draft dodgers don't hang around here long. They all head for Toronto. That's Canada's Sodom and Gomorrah."

"Would you like a coffee, Mister Perle?" Brill asked, preparing for the trickiest part of this conversation.

"No, thank you," Perle said.

Leaning toward the journalist, Brill lowered his voice and said, "Mister Perle, I want to tell you about the perps I'm pursuing. They're not your run-of-the-mill draft dodgers. They're also suspects in the cold-blooded murder of four men – and they're passing counterfeit money. Degenerates like this are a danger to the public and they're in *your* country now." Brill paused, letting that sink in. "Putting men like this away is a duty that goes beyond red tape and bleeding heart directives. I'm hoping that through your work, you've met officials with the courage to do what's right."

Perle nodded. "I have some sources who might be willing to help you," he said. "What do you have in mind?"

"I'm certain these perps crossed from Detroit into Windsor over the last two days. I need to see the security tapes from the Windsor border station to get some hard evidence that will put them away."

Perle rose to his feet. "I admire your devotion to justice, Mister Brill," he said. "I'll make some calls and let you know."

# 43

**"THAT'S THEM,"** Brill said, looking into the video monitor. The paused black-and-white image was grainy. But Sheri Jean's descriptions of Cruiser and Peanut fit this pair perfectly, right down to the bruised forehead on the little one. Brill looked at the time log on the screen. They'd crossed the border less than 24 hours ago.

The station captain pointed through the window to an officer typing in the next room. "My sergeant remembers one of them was born in Cuba. That's the reason they were stopped," he explained. "Their IDs checked out. No warrants on any of them. Unfortunately, we're not allowed to make copies of their documents."

Brill gritted his teeth. *A spic? My God, how rotten could these two get?* After composing himself, Brill pointed to the third hippie on the screen. "Any idea who this is?"

"My men have seen him here before. He's a local. Brings draft dodgers across all the time," the station captain said. "It galls me that our hands are tied."

"This video technology is exceptional, Captain. Not many places in the States have anything like this yet," Brill said. "Hopefully, the day will come when you can really put it to use."

"In the meantime, I'm glad to know I can help you nab these mugs, Mister Brill."

"Can you create still prints from these videos?"

The captain shook his head. "Look, Mister Brill. I've

taken a big risk just showing you these tapes. There are pinkos in this division who would love to destroy my career. Getting their hands on unauthorized prints would make that a cakewalk for them."

"I understand, Captain. You've been a big help with the case. I'm glad Mister Perle put us in touch."

"I wish you luck hunting down these creeps," the captain said. "But please keep in mind, if I'm ever asked, none of this ever happened."

# 44

**COOKIE BEAMED** at Peanut like Timmy's mother on *Lassie* as she pressed the elevator button for the 7th floor. "Let me do the talking, okay?" she said. "This is the best opening for a Sevak in the building. Most of the members of this ashram are loaded. They just had somebody move out and they want to put a Sevak in that room instead of another student."

Peanut looked bummed. "Cruiser and me will have to share a room?"

"Afraid so," Cookie said.

"Hey," I said, suddenly pissed. "I'm not so hot about living with you either, shithead."

Cookie touched Peanut's cheek. "I'm only two floors away, babe. You can crash with me anytime."

The invitation didn't surprise me. Actually, I was surprised Cookie had found time to set this whole thing up. She'd spent all of last night and most of today in her room broiling the *salchicha* with Peanut.

"You really think we'll get this gig?" I asked.

"I won't kid you," Cookie said. "This isn't going to be easy. No ashram here has ever hired a pair of Sevaks."

"These are open minded people, right?" I said. "I mean, innovation is a good thing."

"The students in this ashram are a busy bunch," Cookie said. "They need a Sevak who knows what to do without being told. Think you two are up to that?"

"Cruiser will figure out all that organizing shit," Peanut said. "My job will be kicking ass."

"What about pay?" I asked.

"They won't pay double, that's for sure," Cookie answered. "Let's see how this goes. We can sort out the pay if they like you," she said. Then she added, "One final thing. Tell the truth about anything they ask."

Once the elevator doors opened, we followed Cookie down the hall to a door marked 7-C. After Cookie knocked and the door opened, my jaw almost hit the floor.

Standing in the doorway was the green-eyed goddess I'd seen downstairs last night. She looked even better up close.

"Hi, Cookie. Come in," she said, then led us past a small, messy kitchen.

I could not keep my eyes off her. She had the kind of full curves Cuban males find irresistible.

We entered a small living area and found a group of people, nicely dressed but definitely freaks.

Cookie introduced everyone. There were eight members of the ashram. Only one of their names stuck with me.

Elise.

As interviews go, this was certainly low stress. They asked Peanut and me about the music we liked, the food we ate, and what kind of dope we did. Both of us told the truth.

When the group ran out of questions, Elise looked at Cookie and said, "Everyone here trusts you, Cookie. You're the best Sevak in the building. If you vouch for these guys, I think we might be willing to try them out for a while." Elise then scanned the faces around her. They nodded in agreement.

The next day, Peanut and I became Sevaks of Ashram 7-C.

# 45

**I WAS** into the second chapter of *Soul on Ice* when Elise and Kazuo walked into my room in the ashram.

"Cruiser, Kazuo is very disappointed," Elise said. "He asked for green tea and you stocked the cupboard with black tea."

Cringing, I put down the book. This was Peanut's fuck up. In our Sevak deal, I made the grocery lists and Peanut did the shopping. My list had said green tea.

"I'm sorry, Kazuo. I promise we'll be more careful next time," I said, silently cursing the little shit.

"You need to pay attention," Kazuo said sternly, then huffed out of the room.

Elise smiled. "Kazuo can be blunt sometimes. Don't take it personally," she said, then started to leave.

"Wait," I said, rising to my feet. "You're very kind, Elise. Not a lot of bosses are."

"I'm not the boss here, Cruiser. This is a collective."

I stepped closer to her and smiled. "Well, you could rule my heart anytime, you know."

Instead of the usual flirty laugh I'd get for a line like that, Elise's smile faded. "I'm afraid I'll have to abdicate," she said, then left.

I watched her walk away. I'd struck out again.

After a week into this whole Sevak thing, I was having second thoughts.

Peanut was spending most of his time rocking the bed

springs in Cookie's room, leaving me on duty alone at our ashram.

But what could I do about it? Cookie had gotten us the job – and she was our source for free weed.

Meanwhile, our ashram mates seemed nuttier than a bag of trail mix.

Kazuo was a conceptual artist. His latest work was a series of letters from a fictional art critic named Jacqueline Flowers who wrote about exhibits that didn't exist.

Janet was a lesbian who took pictures of herself half naked wearing masks she made from feathers. Peanut was a big fan of her work.

Gary and Larry shared a room and were producing a documentary on urban bird habitats.

Jacques was a math whiz studying something called fractals. The rest of us didn't have a clue what the hell that was.

And then there was Elise.

My green-eyed goddess kept busier than anyone else in the ashram. She led several groups in Latin American Studies and tutored other students. After sitting through a couple of her classes, I knew this was the woman for me.

I wouldn't have to hide being into books with Elise. She was as nerdy as I was – and hotter than a lunch in Jalisco.

Along with being smart and beautiful, Elise had a fire in the belly I lacked.

Cookie told me why Elise worked so hard. Unlike the others in the ashram, her family was not rich. So Elise dealt some killer weed on the side to bankroll her studies.

This was the love trifecta for me.

Finding myself in Elise's ashram had seemed like a dream at first. But I'd hit a wall of ice every time I'd tried to get somewhere with her. I tried compliments. Brought her snacks. Left cute notes. Nothing worked.

And the more she shot me down, the more I fell in love.

# 46

**THE ALARM** on the motel room's nightstand rang at noon.

Brill got out of bed, took care of business in the bathroom, then studied his face in the mirror.

After three days without a shave, he was ready for work.

He'd never gone undercover before. He was a motives and evidence guy. Putting on a getup and pretending to be someone else seemed unsavory somehow. In his mind, there was a reason thespian rhymed with lesbian. Still, the perps in this case were so heinous, he was willing to go slumming – quite literally.

Posing as a bum would give him a chance to scour Toronto's Yorkville district without being spotted. Every city seemed to have a hippie hellhole these days. Finding Toronto's had not taken long.

Finding the time to pursue this case had been harder. His boss would not have sanctioned this foray into Canada. So he'd taken personal leave – which he had plenty of. Brill hated vacations.

After donning the ratty clothes he'd gotten at a thrift shop, Brill pulled on a knit cap and headed for his first day undercover.

# 47

**COMMUNAL LIFE** will test your patience.

With ten of us sharing a bathroom, mornings were a bitch. I usually waited until everyone was gone to take my shower – and hoped for luck on enough hot water.

So I was surprised when I heard crockery breaking in the kitchen. I thought I was alone. The smashing continued as I dried off and left the bathroom with a towel around my waist.

Reaching the kitchen, I saw Peanut with a hammer in his hand. He reached into the cupboard and pulled out a bowl, then held it over the garbage can and shattered it.

"What the hell are you doing?" I said.

"Cookie told me the assholes here are complaining to Elise about dirty dishes in the sink," he said, taking down another bowl and breaking it. "That's the last one," he said.

"The last of what?"

"The reason the dishes pile up in the sink here is because we have too many," Peanut said. "Now we only have four sets. Only four people can eat here at a time anyway. So they want to eat? They gotta wash dishes."

I thought about it. The little shit was right.

When Elise returned to the ashram for lunch, she agreed. "That was a novel solution. I guess Cookie knew what she was doing when she recommended you, Peanut."

So Peanut, who spent most of his time away from our

ashram with Cookie, was Elise's hero.

There seemed to be no way I could catch a break with her.

That night, after Elise invited Peanut and me into her room, I got the feeling things might get even worse.

Elise's face was tight as she spoke. "Look, I know you two have only been here a couple of weeks. But I'm sorry. I don't know how much longer I can afford my share of your pay."

I nodded, trying not to panic. "Do you mind if I ask why?"

"There are more people dealing weed in Rochdale every day. It's eating into my business. I'd need to cut back on my study projects to find new customers – and I don't want to do that."

"Have you talked to the others in the ashram about this?" I asked.

"Yes. They want to keep you. But not if I can't pay my share."

I stared at the floor, totally bummed.

"Hey," Peanut said. "What if I help you deal? I've got the time. Being a Sevak's not a nine-to-five job or anything."

Yeah, for *him* it certainly wasn't, I told myself.

Elise's eyebrows rose. "I hadn't thought of that," she said. "But I'm not sure how that would work."

"You can front me the weed," Peanut said. "My take of the sales would go toward paying me and Cruiser. With me bringing in new customers and you keeping the old ones, there's no way you won't come out ahead."

"I don't like this idea," I said. We were out of the woods on all the shit back in Kentucky. I didn't want to jump into more trouble here. I couldn't say this in front of

Elise, though.

Peanut sneered. "Cruiser, you're such a chickenshit. There's not much chance of getting caught dealing around here. The cops would need to park a fleet of buses down Bloor to haul away all the freaks selling weed at Rochdale."

"No, but they can sure as hell bust the careless ones," I said. "You've never sold dope before, Peanut."

"C'mon, man," he said. "I'll be careful."

I shook my head. "Your idea of being careful is driving under a hundred when you're totally stoned."

"Tell you what," Peanut said. "If I've got a deal with anybody outside Rochdale, I'll let you and Elise decide if it's too risky."

I was stunned when I heard Elise say, "That sounds reasonable to me. This might work."

Looking into those green eyes, I felt myself weaken. This might finally be my chance to win Elise over. "All right. I'm in," I said, certain that my gonads were getting the better of my brain.

# 48

**BRILL ENTERED** his motel room and headed straight for the Jack Daniels.

Pouring out a shot, he downed it and let out a long, breathy sigh.

This was a day to celebrate. He'd finally spotted one of them – the little one called Peanut.

The runt had been walking down Bloor Street carrying a couple of grocery bags. Keeping his distance, Brill had trailed him until Peanut entered a high-rise known as Rochdale College.

One of the magazines he'd read in his ongoing research had called the place a vertical Haight-Ashbury. The article also said this experimental college was North America's largest drug distribution warehouse.

Looking back, he probably should have started his surveillance there. This was a perfect hideout for sleazeballs like Cruiser and Peanut. The grocery bags the runt had been carrying were probably filled with maryjane.

Brill's research had revealed that "maryjane" was hippie lingo for marijuana – by far their most popular drug.

After nearly three weeks undercover, finding Peanut had come with little time to spare. His leave from work would be used up soon.

But one good thing had come from the delay. He'd had time to plan his next move once he spotted one of the dirtbags.

He had no authority to arrest Cruiser and Peanut in Canada. But his ace-in-the-hole was getting the Mounties to pick them up for a local crime. The warrant and extradition papers would be a cinch once these two were in custody. As a bonus, he could also charge them with evading the draft once he got them back on U.S. soil.

The obvious rap to nab them on was drugs.

He'd already bought the clothes he'd use for his next undercover role.

He could hardly pass for a hippie. But the identity he'd chosen would not be hard to pull off: a rich author looking for a big maryjane score.

He'd alert the Mounties and have them on backup as he made the dope deal. Once he had the perps on the hook, the Mounties would swoop in and make the arrest.

Brill poured himself another jack. His complete ritual would be especially satisfying tonight.

# 49

**I OPENED** the kitchen cupboard, still not used to the smell.

I'd grown up with a whiff of garlic and cumin coming from the shelves. The food cabinets in our ashram smelled more like insecticide.

The cupboard had stuff I never knew people ate: dried seaweed, soybeans, spirulina, wheat germ and granola. My groove was hamburger helper and instant pudding, man.

As Sevak, my job was stocking the kitchen for everyone else – and I needed to make some room in the cupboard. Peanut was out shopping and would be coming back soon with new groceries.

Making space in the fridge, I rearranged packages of tofu, bean sprouts, and tempeh – more stuff I'd never eaten before. But I was getting used to it. They have a saying about food in Cuba: If it doesn't kill, it's nourishment.

I heard the door into the ashram open.

Peanut was beaming as he walked into the kitchen and put down the grocery bags. "We've got a whale, man!" he said.

"Somebody here will probably eat it," I said. "There's nothing too weird for this bunch."

"I'm not shitting you, Cruiser. I found a guy who wants to buy a half-pound of weed."

My paranoia radar flipped on. "Where?"

"About a block from here."

"You mean some guy you just met on the street?"

"Well, yeah. His name is Eric."

"This is exactly what I was afraid of, Peanut. You have no idea if this guy's a narc."

"Hey, man," Peanut said, getting pissed. "That's why I'm telling you like I promised. I'm going to tell Elise about this guy, too."

I could see Peanut was sure this was legit. I hoped Elise would not agree.

"Help me get this stuff put away," I said. "We'll talk to Elise tonight. And tell Cookie I think she should be in on this, too."

# 50

**THAT NIGHT,** the four of us met in Elise's room.

Although we were all sitting on the floor with our backs against the wall, the conversation had taken on the vibe of a courtroom. There was no doubt that Elise was the judge.

"What did this guy look like?" I asked Peanut.

"Bald, kinda short and chubby. Nice threads. He looked like he had some coin. He said his name was Eric without me asking him."

"Tell me exactly what he said," I asked.

"He said 'I'm looking to buy some maryjane. Do you know where I can get some?' Then I said, 'How much?' and he said 'A half-pound.'"

"He actually called it maryjane?"

"Yeah," Peanut said. "He's not a freak, Cruiser. The guy is old. Like forty or something."

Cookie spoke up. "Cruiser, narcs are smart. They don't use old geezers for undercover work."

"So what happened then?" I asked.

"I was all cagey, you know?" Peanut said. "I asked him why he wanted that much. And he said he was an author throwing a party for some friends"

"Did you tell Eric you had a half-pound of weed to sell?"

"I'm not stupid, Cruiser. I told Eric I might know some-one willing to sell the weed and I'd check it out for him."

"So what did you two agree to do?"

"Eric said he'd meet me at the statue in front of our building tomorrow night at ten. If I had something to sell, he'd have the money."

I didn't like the sound of this at all. If Peanut got busted, he wouldn't rat out any of us. I was sure of that. But the police report could still get back to the States. And that would mean the American heat might figure out I was in Toronto, too.

"Did you and Eric agree on a price?" I asked.

"Yeah. I told him a hundred bucks," Peanut said. "I figured at ten bucks a lid, a half-pound would be eighty bucks. Then I added an extra twenty 'cause Eric looked like he could afford it."

"I like the way you do math, babe," Cookie said, patting Peanut's leg.

I looked at Elise. "Do you think a hundred bucks is worth the risk?"

Elise gave that some thought for a moment. "I'd miss a lot of academic time hustling ten lids," she said.

"See," Peanut said to me, "I told you she'd agree."

I still wasn't convinced this deal was safe. Something didn't feel right. But Peanut had won over Cookie by showing some balls. If I was going to get anywhere with Elise, maybe I needed to step up, too.

"I have an idea," I said. "I'll do this deal with Eric myself."

"Why do you think that's a good idea?" Elise asked.

After I explained my plan, they all agreed.

# 51

**AT TEN** sharp, I walked out the front door of Rochdale. Sitting near a plate glass window, Elise, Cookie and Peanut were watching me on the sly.

My throat was tight. They were trusting me to decide whether we made a deal with Eric that would fatten all our wallets or put us behind bars.

The guy standing under the streetlamp by the courtyard's statue fit Peanut's description of Eric – but not my idea of an author.

Not that my pond was very deep on that subject. What I thought an author should look like came from the back cover of books. Most of the living ones dressed like frumps.

This guy's tweed jacket with elbow patches and white ascot looked like the costume for somebody playing Henry Higgins in a high school production of Pygmalion. (I know because I played Freddy in ours.)

Still, I wasn't sure. Maybe this was how Canadian authors dressed.

Eric didn't seem surprised to see me. "Where's Peanut?" he asked.

"He's busy," I said smiling. "Anyway, I wanted to do this. I've never met a real author before, man."

"I see you've got my maryjane there," he said, nodding toward the rolled-up grocery bag in my hand.

"Yeah, I do. But, like, what are some of the books you've written, man?"

"Look, I think that's getting a little personal. Let's keep this on a first name basis, all right?"

"Sure, man. I get it," I said, raising my palm. "But can you at least tell me if you write fiction or non-fiction?"

"Fiction. Non-Fiction. I write both."

"That is so far out!" I said. "See, I want to write someday, too. And I'm wondering something. How do you feel about switching from first person point of view to third person in the same paragraph?"

The look in Eric's eyes told me he had no fucking clue what I was talking about.

"Doing that is okay, I suppose. Sometimes," Eric finally said.

"Wow. That's good to know, man," I said, putting my hand behind my back and wiggling a "no" with my finger to Elise, Cookie and Peanut.

"So," Eric said. "Are we going to do this or not?"

"Sure, man," I said, then handed him the bag.

"Here's your money," he said, reaching into his jacket.

"You might want to check out your goods before you pay me."

Eric's mouth fell open as he looked in the bag. "What's this," he said pulling out one of the penny candies inside.

"Your Mary Janes, man."

The look on that undercover cop's face as he dropped the bag made me feel like I'd won *La Bolita*. Just as I thought. This whole thing was a sting. My plan had worked like a—

"You're under arrest," the cop said putting his hand on my shoulder and pulling handcuffs from his coat.

I stepped back and tore away from his grip. "Arrest me for what? Selling candy?"

"You're wanted for murder in Kentucky."

My *huevos* retracted like landing gear as two cops in uniform ran up to us.

"We'll take over now, Mister Brill," the older cop said.

"Is this the evidence?" the young uniform asked, picking up the bag.

The plainclothes cop's face went scarlet as the uniformed guys looked inside.

They doubled over laughing.

"There's nothing funny, here," the plainclothes said. "This thug is wanted for murder, counterfeiting and evading the draft."

"We made it clear, Mister Brill. Unless there's evidence of a crime committed in our jurisdiction, we can't arrest anyone without a warrant."

The older uniform looked at me and said, "You're free to go."

I was too stunned to move for a moment.

Trying to keep my knees from wobbling, I finally turned around.

Feeling the eyes of the cops on my back, I walked into the building and passed by Elise, Cookie and Peanut without looking at them. Stepping into the usual evening crowd, I felt safe enough to look behind me. The cops were gone.

I waited by the elevators until the other three caught up with me.

Elise took my face in her hands and kissed me. "You surprised me tonight, Cruiser," she said. "There's more to you than hormones."

# 52

**"WHAT HAPPENED** out there, Cruiser?" Elise asked after the four of us were in her room. "It seemed like you were about to get busted, then they let you go."

My plan had been for Peanut to bring the weed outside if I signaled Eric seemed legit. Otherwise, I'd hand Eric the Mary Janes.

I looked at Peanut. Reading my mind, he nodded. It was time to come clean.

"We're not really draft dodgers," I said. Then I told them the whole story: the Mustang, the murders, the counterfeit money, and how it brought us to Detroit, then to Windsor, and finally to Rochdale. "I think this guy Eric is some kind of an American cop. When he saw we were on to his drug bust, he tried to arrest me for the murders in Kentucky. But the local cops wouldn't let him do it. They said he needed a warrant."

"That makes sense," Elise said. "Extradition treaties are part of my classes. The drug bust was an excuse for getting you into custody. The U.S. cop probably didn't have an extradition order yet."

Peanut touched Cookie's hand. "I'm sorry we didn't tell you the truth. We thought you wouldn't believe us."

Cookie grabbed Peanut and pulled him against her. "You're a tough little squirt," she said, "But I know you're not a killer."

I looked at Elise like a pooch begging for a biscuit.

The treat she tossed was tiny. "I can't see you doing that either, Cruiser," Elise said.

"You and Cruiser can't stay here, babe," Cookie said to Peanut. "You aren't safe at Rochdale anymore."

Elise agreed. "It's only a matter of time until the U.S. cop gets that warrant. And now he knows where to find you. You guys need to book."

"I can get you both to Manitoba," Cookie said. "My family has a farm there."

"They should split up, Cookie," Elise said. "These two together are easy to spot."

Peanut and I looked at each other. I could see he didn't want to split up either.

"We could travel to Manitoba separately," I said.

"Yeah," Peanut agreed. "That would work, wouldn't it?"

"There may be another way out of this for you, Cruiser," Elise said. "Would you like to hear about it?"

For ten years, the little shit and I had been like peanut butter and jelly. But there was a hint of promise in Elise's offer I couldn't ignore.

"What have you got in mind?" I asked.

# 53

**AFTER SCANNING** the alley for cops, Elise and I left Rochdale by the back door.

We cut through parking lots and lawns, staying in the shadows and out of the streetlights, making it hard for anyone to follow us.

I thought it was a little too much cloak and dagger shit, but Elise had insisted I shave my goat, put a scarf over my hair and borrow one of Cookie's coats – which was a couple of sizes too big. Walking beside Elise, we looked like a tall babushka and her granddaughter.

I still couldn't believe this was happening. When Elise had told me this morning how I could get out of this jam, I almost shit.

She thought I should return to Cuba.

Elise leaned close to me as we walked and said, "Look, Cruiser. I can see you're reluctant. Are you absolutely sure you have no political issues with this?"

"I'm cool with the whole thing in Cuba. Bitching about things down there is my dad's hang-up,"

"So why are you dragging your feet?"

I couldn't bring myself to tell the truth. I didn't want to leave Toronto. I wanted to stay here with her.

"I don't know. I guess I'm not sure about all the details of getting there."

"Okay," she said as we reached a stone building with a metal plaque that read: School of Theology - Faculty

Offices. "Father Pat will clear things up for you. He's connected to the cause all over the world, Cruiser. He helped Daniel Berrigan when he was on the lam."

Walking up to a heavy wooden door, I asked, "How do you know this guy?"

"My father was working for Jamaica at the UN when he met Father Pat. I've known him since I was a girl."

"What did your father do at the UN?"

"Shuffled papers, mostly," she said, stepping inside the door.

I took off the scarf as we entered a dimly lit hallway. Every door was closed – except for one near the end throwing a pizza slice of light into the corridor.

"What's your father do now?" I asked as she started toward the open door.

"He died when I was in high school."

"Wow, that's a bummer, I'm sorry."

"Thanks," Elise said softly as we walked. "Look, Cruiser. I know you're not sure about doing this. But the risks go up every hour you're still here. If you say no to Father Pat's help tonight, there won't be a second chance. The hotter you get, the greater the danger becomes for him."

I nodded. "I appreciate what you're doing, Elise. I really do."

The open door at the end of the hallway was marked "Fr. Patrick Harrington." We stopped and peered inside.

Father Pat was not what I expected.

On the phone behind a small desk was a slim middle aged guy with short gray hair rocking flannels and jeans. But it was his eyes that really struck me. I can't tell you why, but they seemed strong and gentle at the same time.

Father Pat put his palm over the receiver and said, "I'm

sorry. Can you give me a few minutes?"

"Of course," Elise said and closed the door.

After stepping away to give Father Pat some privacy, we stood quietly in the darkened hall.

"I guess we're both half orphans," I said softly, after a moment.

"What do you mean?"

"My mom died when I was born. My dad raised me by himself."

"My parents divorced when I was four. I lived with my dad until he died."

"Does your mother live in Toronto?" I asked.

"No, she's in Nova Scotia. We're not very close."

"I'm not too tight with my father either," I said. "Why don't you get along with your mom?"

"She's a tight-assed white girl who had a fling with a black dude in college – and regretted it ever since."

"That's pretty heavy, Elise."

"Look, Cruiser," she said, touching my sleeve. "Not a lot of people at Rochdale know about this. You understand?"

Before I could answer, the door opened, lighting up the hallway.

"Come in," Father Pat said, waving for us to sit on the chairs in front of his desk.

"Elise explained your situation," he said. "We'll need to handle this delicately. Do you have the information I asked for?"

"Yes," I said, handing him the folded sheet I'd been carrying in my pocket.

Elise had asked me to write down my full name and my date and place of birth, along with everything I could recall about my relatives in Cuba.

Father Pat looked over the sheet for a couple of minutes. "This should work," he said. "You'll need to get a haircut, Nestor. Cuba is going through an unfortunate overreaction toward foreign influences right now. They're not very fond of hippies," he said with a soft smile, "but they still welcome Cubans returning to their *patria*."

I still wasn't sure about all this. Elise seemed to sense it.

"The U.S. authorities can't touch you in Cuba, Cruiser. It's the only place you'll be safe."

"Elise is right, son. Time is not on your side. Once they have an extradition warrant, every Mountie post in Canada will be looking for you," he said. "The cliché is that the Mounties always get their man. I wouldn't recommend testing it."

I swallowed hard and nodded.

Father Pat held up something that looked like a passport. "If you return to Cuba, you'll arrive with a Residence Permit for Statelessness like this. It's not a passport and that could get awkward when you arrive. But eventually, someone with authority will approve it."

Or I could rot in jail if they didn't. That sounded pretty sketchy.

"Father Pat's group will arrange for your air travel and cover the costs," Elise said.

"I know this is not an easy decision, Nestor," Father Pat said. "But I have to know tonight. We'll need a photo of you as soon as possible – with a haircut."

I sat there, petrified. Did I have the balls to do this? Then again, it would take some balls to stay. There was only one way I could decide.

"Father, is it okay if I talk to Elise in the hallway?"

He smiled. "Sure."

Once we were alone in the hall, I said, "Elise, if there's any chance that you'd ever—"

She touched my lips. "Stop," she said. "I wouldn't be doing all of this if I wasn't fond of you, Cruiser. But don't you see? The most caring thing I can do is to make sure you're safe," she said, cradling my face. "So, please. Go."

# 54

**BRILL SMUDGED** his finger on the carbon paper as he yanked the triplicate sheets out of the Selectric.

"Fucking paperwork," he muttered to himself. The report he'd just finished had been a pain in the ass of the highest order.

On his first day back in the Louisville office, Brill had expected a normal return to work after a vacation. Instead, he found the office buzzing with hot scuttlebutt.

The Mounties had filed a report with the Bureau office in DC about his attempted bust in Toronto. The fucking pinko Canucks had ratted him out.

*No good deed goes unpunished,* Brill told himself as he tossed his report of the Paducah murder investigation into the OUT basket on his desk.

# 55

**ELISE LEANED** into the doorway of our room in the ashram.

"It's better if you two say goodbye here," she whispered, then left Peanut and me alone.

We both knew what Elise meant. A teary farewell in public might create attention we didn't need.

I zipped up Pancho and said, "Man, I thought this shit would be over when we hit Toronto."

"Yeah. It's a fucking bummer, man."

"Well, at least you found someone, bro. I'm happy for you and Cookie."

"Thanks, Cruiser. I wish it could have worked out for you and Elise."

"I don't know," I said, with a dry laugh. "Getting tight with Elise would have made leaving here even harder."

"You could just stay and keep wearing women's clothes, you know," he said, grinning.

"Sure," I said, chuckling. "I can hear Greta now. *'Oh, Cruiser. You finally came out of the closet, honey!'*" I said, imitating Greta's swishy voice.

Peanut giggled. "Naw. Greta would get all jealous of you... *'Bitch, you try to outshine me on Halloween and I'll scratch your fucking eyes out!'*" he shrieked before we both doubled over laughing.

Slowly, our laughter drained away.

"I'm gonna miss Greta," I said, dabbing the corner of my eye.

"Yeah. Me too," he said, wiping his cheek.

I looked at Peanut and sighed. "I left my family in Cuba never expecting to see them again. Now, I'm going back there," I said. "You never know what might happen, Maxwell. You just never know."

I hugged the little shit, picked up Pancho, and walked out of the room.

I didn't want him to see me cry.

# 56

**"I'LL BE** there," Brill said in a tight voice, then hung up the phone.

The call he'd been dreading since returning to work had come.

Like a steam locomotive leaving the station, Brill's anger grew with each step he took toward his boss's office.

Brill knew Calvin Price would pile on now that he was down. And his boss wasn't alone. This whole division was full of mediocrities who shunned him because he didn't fit the slim and dapper Zimmie look the Director favored for his agents. The Mounties' report to DC had given them the excuse they'd been waiting for.

*Fuck them all,* Brill told himself as he knocked on Calvin Price's door.

"Come in," his boss called out. "Take a seat," he said once Brill was inside.

Pulse throbbing in his ears, Brill dropped into the chair before Price's desk.

Calvin Price had been promoted ahead of him several years before.

In Jack's mind, Price was a goldbrick EEOC hire. Brill thought the Bureau had gone down the crapper when they started pushing aside white males in favor of less qualified people to fill quotas. Brill had not been shy in sharing his anger about this bias against whites. So Jack had always assumed Price hated him.

Brill gritted his teeth. This wasn't a real post-mortem of his case with the two hippie scumbags. This was a trap by a guy who wanted to remove a better-qualified rival.

"I can't comment about your numerous violations of protocols in Canada, Jack. An internal board of inquiry is already looking into that," Price said, folding his hands.

Brill nodded, drumming the arm of his chair.

"But I'm going to give it to you straight, Jack. You made the Bureau look like clowns up there. You went undercover without authorization – or even any field experience. Now I hear the Mounties are calling it the Penny Candy Pinch," Price said, shaking his head. "What the hell led you to Canada in the first place?"

"Those perps belong behind bars, Cal. We both know that. I should be commended for showing initiative, not get crucified."

"You still haven't answered my question. Why were you in Canada?"

Brill rolled his eyes. "It's in my report."

"I want to hear it from *you*."

"Along with the murder and counterfeiting charges, those two were draft dodgers," Brill said, jutting out his chin.

"What made you think they were draft dodgers?"

"A musician who rode the bus to Detroit with them gave me that impression."

"How did you locate this musician?"

"I checked the local clubs in Detroit."

Price flipped through Brill's report, then looked up. "Says here you were in Detroit for less than a day. How many clubs did you check before you found this musician?"

"Three," Brill said, tugging at his collar.

Price's eyebrows rose. "There must be dozens of clubs in Detroit. How did you locate this musician so quickly?"

Brill squirmed in his chair. "A source I've trusted for a long time led me to him."

"Who is the source?"

Brill folded his arms. "I need to protect my source's confidentiality."

"Jack, you know the Bureau's guidelines. You're required to reveal the identity of a CI when requested by a superior," Price said calmly. "I'll guarantee your informant's confidentiality. But I have to verify this information."

"The source's name is Henry."

"Is that a first or last name?" Price said, writing on a yellow legal pad.

"That's his only name," Brill said, feeling his face redden. "Anyway, that's what I call him. I don't know his real name."

"Where does Henry live?" Price asked, pen poised to write.

"He moves around a lot."

"How do you get in touch with him?"

"Look, I know you and a lot of others around here have hated me for a long time," Brill snarled. "But I still solve more cases than anyone else, don't I?"

"That's irrelevant," Price said, trying to stay calm. "How do you get in touch with this Henry?"

Brill took a deep breath, then said, "I usually open something."

Price scowled. "All right, Jack. Cut the bullshit. You either tell me about this informant or you can tack perjury on to your inquiry when it reaches the board."

"I'm not lying, goddamit," Brill insisted. "Henry turns up when I open something."

"Open something?"

"Yeah, like a can. Or a door. Sometimes it's a faucet."

Price's eyebrows knitted. "What does Henry look like?"

"I don't actually see him. He's more of a voice."

"A voice?"

"Yeah, and he's cracked a lot of cases for me," Brill said, getting louder, eyes glaring. "Henry also tipped me off that these perps were Manson copycats."

Price put down his pen and slowly leaned back in his chair. "I see. I think I get the picture here," he said in a voice you'd use with a four-year-old. "Thank you, Jack. That'll be all for now."

Brill rose to his feet. "I'm not making this up!" he yelled. "Henry talks to me all the time. I can prove it."

Brill picked up a manila folder from Price's desk and opened it. "Henry?" he asked, eyes circling the room.

Grabbing Price's thermos jug, Brill unscrewed the top. "Henry?"

Price rose and stepped back in shock as Brill walked around the desk and opened a drawer. "C'mon, Henry. I need to hear from you, goddamit!" he shouted.

Price backed away, making his way slowly toward the door.

"I know he'll talk to me," Brill said, opening a file cabinet. "He always does eventually."

Reaching the door, Price opened it partway. "Get security up here. Right away," he whispered to the assistant seated just outside his office.

"Henry? Henry?" Brill said, opening the window shades.

# 57

**I'D FORGOTTEN** what the ocean looked like from the air.

For most of the flight from Toronto, we'd passed over land – a lot of it covered in clouds. But when we reached the Keys, everything below my window changed. The glittering water turned more shades of blue and green than I knew existed.

For the umpteenth time, I rubbed the back of my neck where my hair used to be. Everything about me felt different.

Everything except my jonesing for Elise.

With my hair short and face shaved, Elise and I figured it was safe enough to jump into a cab outside Rochdale and ride to the airport together. Neither of us said much on the way there. Although I'd seen very little of Toronto, my eyes stayed on Elise.

Our silence continued in the terminal as I picked up my ticket.

Finally, it was time to board the plane.

"Thank you, Elise," I mumbled. "For everything."

"Be safe, Cruiser," she said, then walked away.

Watching her leave, I was surprised. I wasn't feeling any pain. I felt something worse.

Empty.

Staring down into the water outside my window, I looked for a green that matched the color of her eyes.

I couldn't find it.

"We're on our approach for landing," the pilot's voice said over the intercom. "Please fasten your seat belts."

# 58

**GAZING TOWARD** the horizon, I saw a hazy strip of land through the window. My heart began to thump.

My seat was just behind the jet's wing. So my first view of Havana in ten years was like watching a movie on a screen with a bent corner.

Right away, I recognized *El Malecón*, the seawall at the edge of the city. Following the curving seawall, I spotted the opening into the bay and *El Morro*, the lighthouse you always see on Cuban postcards.

Some of the buildings were familiar. The Havana Hilton, a concrete and glass Hershey-bar renamed *Habana Libre* after the revolution... the dome of the *capitolio*, which looks pretty much like the U.S. capitol in Washington... the tall tapering monument to Jose Martí that Cubans nicknamed the *rallador* – the grater... and the *Palacio Deportivo* that looked like the arrival of the huge-ass flying saucer from *The Day the Earth Stood Still*.

This was my first time to see the place I was born from the air. On my flight to Miami when I was a kid, we hadn't flown over the city.

I'd boarded the plane in Toronto through a jetway. In Havana, we got out of the plane right onto the tarmac. My first sensation setting foot on *mi patria* was heat. I mean, serious fucking heat, man.

After being chilled to the bone up north, I thought I'd welcome the warmth. But the sky was cloudy, and the air so thick, walking toward the terminal was like wading through a bowl of *caldo gallego*.

I was sweating by the time we were led into a large building marked *Inmigración y Aduana*. A half-dozen ceiling fans hung idle overhead. I didn't think I could sweat anymore until I caught sight of the wall of tiny booths ahead of me.

Behind a yellow stripe painted on the concrete, the passengers were forming lines in front of eight narrow doors. People were going in, one-by-one for some kind of interrogation or something.

When my turn came, I entered the little booth shivering like I was back on the road to Toronto.

Behind a chest-high counter sat a young woman in a tan military uniform. She had soulful almond eyes and olive skin.

"May I see your passport?" she said in Spanish. Her accent was from the eastern side of the island. Like me, most Cubans in Miami spoke Spanish with an accent unique to Havana.

"I don't have a passport. I'm traveling using a Residence Permit for Statelessness from Canada," I croaked, putting the permit on the counter.

She looked at my document like someone just told her she had herpes. She sighed and said, "Wait here," then disappeared through the booth's back door carrying my permit.

I was about to shit a brick by the time a short guy with an Errol Flynn mustache stepped into the booth. "Who prepared this permit for you?"

Would I be ratting out Father Pat if I told the truth? "A priest in Toronto," I said, trying to be cagy.

"Would that be Father Patrick Harrington?"

Oh, shit. The jig was up. There was no point in lying now. "Yes," I said grudgingly, waiting for the guards to appear.

"Everything is in order here," he said. "You can proceed to Customs."

I walked out of that booth making a promise to myself. If they still had churches in this country, I was going to light a candle for that priest.

# 59

**BY THE** time my taxi reached the Luyano district where my aunt and uncle lived, it was full-on nighttime.

Traffic was light. But the streets were teeming. People sat on stoops and balconies, others strolled around or grooved to the music blaring from the windows.

The scruffy flat-roofed buildings lining the street were mostly three stories high. Painted in a clash of faded colors, they looked like a shelf of broken-down books.

When my cab pulled up to an ancient four-floor walk-up, my aunt and uncle were waving to me from the balcony of their apartment. I'd written to them with the date of my arrival. They must have been waiting up there all day.

Seeing Tia Clara and Tio Lalo again was a total trip. They looked about the same to me. Maybe a little grayer and thinner.

But they were blown away when they set eyes on their full-grown nephew.

After long hugs from both of them, we were all dewy-eyed.

"Thank you for letting me stay with you," I said, looking around their apartment. "I've never forgotten this place." It still smelled like a mix of lard, garlic and Vicks VapoRub.

"I'm happy to see you haven't forgotten your milk tongue," my uncle said.

"Tio, where I grew up in Miami, even the yanquis

speak Spanish," I said, suddenly missing Peanut.

"The food in La Yuma must be as good as they say," my aunt said, taking my hands. "You're already taller than your father."

"And taller than me," Tio Lalo added, smiling. "Sit down, Nestor," he said, waving toward the two frayed chairs in their living room.

"It's true about the food, Tia," I said, settling into one of the chairs. "All the Cuban boys who grew up in Miami are taller than their fathers."

Tia put her hand on my arm. "How is your father?"

I knew she was just being polite. Tia Clara had never warmed up to her brother-in-law. "He's fine and sends his regards." I felt bad about lying. But this was the easiest way to get past a formality for both of us.

"We are so happy you're here, Nestor," she said, then brought down a shoe box from the top of the armoire in the corner. "I've got some pictures you'll want to see. I got them out when I heard you were coming."

For the next hour, Tia Clara regaled me with photos of her and my mom growing up... first communions... quinceañeras...trips to the beach.

I realized something at that moment. My dad must have had pictures of mom. He never showed them to me, though. It probably hurt too much.

I tried to hold it back. But I started to cry.

Tio patted my shoulder. "Don't be ashamed, Nestor. There are times when a man cannot help but cry," he said. Looking at Tia, he said, "I told you it might be better to wait a while before you showed him those, mi amor."

"No, I'm glad to see them. Thank you, Tia," I said, taking her hand.

"We've missed you, Nesi," Tia said, using her pet name for me. She and Tio never had kids, although Tio had a son by his first marriage.

"I've got some things to show you as well, muchacho," Tio said, walking into their bedroom. "Give me a minute."

When he returned, Tio waved me over to the table that served as their dining room. Just past the table was the stove, refrigerator and sink that made up their kitchen. As a little kid, I'd ridden my tricycle up and down the tile floor of this apartment, pretending I was on a racetrack. Now, I realized the whole place was about twelve steps long.

"Your father was a magician with engines," he said, pointing to a photo of my father and Lalo, along with his son Emilio, standing in front of a '52 GMC 450 truck.

"How is Emilio doing? He must be nearly thirty by now," I said.

Lalo's face tightened. "I don't see much of Emilio anymore."

Sensing his tension, I changed the subject. "I remember that truck," I said, smiling. "It was blue and had a 4-cyl with a cranky starter."

"You have a good memory," he said, tousling my hair.

"Do you still have the truck?"

"No," he said, then looked away. "I did my duty and turned over my trucking business to the revolution."

I got the feeling this could be touchy. My dad had left Cuba. My uncle stayed behind. Before I could say anything, Tio spoke again.

"Your father did what he thought best. I've always respected that," he said, tapping the table twice like a judge closing a case.

"You've bored this boy long enough, Lalo," Tia said

with a smile. "He's probably tired after a flight all the way from Canada. Let's get him ready for bed."

From the armoire, Tia pulled out blankets, sheets and a pillow. After a few minutes, she'd made a pallet on the tile floor near the door into the balcony.

"Wait a minute," she said, heading to the kitchen. "You're not ready for bed yet."

She returned with something I'd totally forgotten about: a tin pump attached to a tank of bug repellent called a FLIT gun.

"We don't want any mosquitos or roaches bothering our nephew," she said, pumping the poison mist all around my pallet.

Once she was done, she touched my cheek and said, "Sleep well, Nesi. You're back home."

# 60

**A ROOSTER** crowed.

I opened my eyes and looked at the sky through the balcony. There wasn't a hint of daylight. Sleeping on a couple of blankets over the hard tile floor had been okay at first. I'd arrived dog tired and could have slept on a bed of nails. But by the middle of the night, my bones were aching like an old man's.

When the rooster crowed again, I sat up and sighed.

Looking at Pancho, I said, "A half-million people in this city and they still keep chickens. We're not in Kansas anymore, Toto."

As I watched daylight slowly bleed into the sky, I couldn't help thinking about what I'd left behind.

Peanut was probably on his way to Manitoba with Cookie by now. And Elise? I was sure she'd be busy leading classes and dealing weed again.

I remembered something my father had said often that suddenly made sense.

*Always look ahead, Nestor. What's done is done.*

I heard Tia shuffle into the living room. "When was the last time you had café Cubano?" she asked.

"Never, Tia. I wasn't allowed to drink it as a kid."

She touched her forehead. "Ay, dios mio. I'm getting old. How could I forget?" she said and went into the kitchen.

I walked out to the balcony and looked down the street.

The people walking to work along Avenida Acosta were flowing like a meandering stream. They filled the narrow sidewalks and spilled out into the street - where they dodged a chaotic parade of Russian compacts, Detroit relics, buses, motor scooters, and street vendors pushing handcarts.

"Nesi," Tia called out. "Come into the kitchen."

Waiting for me at the table was a tiny white cup brimming with tan foam.

"Try it," she said.

The taste was something like American coffee - if American coffee had worked out at the gym until it could kick Muhammad Ali's ass.

"Wow," I said, lapsing into English.

Tia looked puzzled. "Wah-oh? What does that mean?"

"It's good, Tia. Very, very good," I said, patting her hand.

She smiled. "Many things are hard to find these days, Nesi. But Cubans always find a way to make good coffee."

A lot of exiles I'd known back in Miami believed the people still in Cuba would rise in revolt against all the shortages.

But now, I wasn't sure that would happen. Not as long as they could still make coffee this good.

# 61

**"NESTOR, WE** need to fix the fence on the baboon cage or they're going to start a conga line with the chimps soon," my boss said.

"I'll take care of it, Santiago," I said, while cutting up an assortment of vegetables to feed the primates.

Yeah, I was working with monkeys again.

When I'd applied for a job at the Ministry of Work and Social Security a month ago, someone had decided that my experience at a pet importer in Miami qualified me to feed and hose out the shit from the cages of an assortment of animals at Havana's *Parque Zoológico Nacional*.

When I got to the baboon cage, I saw what Santiago meant. The back corner of the chain-link fence was coming loose along the bottom.

I'd need to put some food in the front corner to draw Bibby, Zola and her baby Nancy over there while I tightened down the fence.

As I shoved some carrots and malanga through the fence to attract the baboons, a visitor behind me said, "Look, they eat better than we do."

I heard someone make that joke at least once a day. Every time, everyone laughed – because it was about half true.

That was something I'd learned after almost two months back in Cuba.

Things were complicated.

Cubans were issued ration books called *libretas* that let you buy small amounts of food and other stuff each month way below regular prices at government stores – when the goods were available. The *libretas* didn't provide everything you'd need. But they kept you from starving.

Rent was free in Cuba. After the revolution, the government had given Tio and Tia their apartment. They used to rent it when I was a kid. But, although Tio and Tia now owned the apartment, they couldn't sell it.

For young people growing up and looking for their own place to live, this system was a bitch. Tia told me the government had stopped all new housing projects a few years back.

Education and health care were free. But schools and hospitals were always scrounging for supplies.

Like I said, things were complicated.

The amazing thing was that Havana was not dreary. Somehow, most Cubans had figured out how to live with this crazy system and seemed to be enjoying life. Maybe it was just the nature of Cubans to find joy under any circumstances. I don't know.

What I *did* know was that my life here was starting to feel like a rerun of Miami.

I wasn't miserable. But I suspected there was something better for me somewhere else.

# 62

**"THAT ONE** is giving you the eye, Nestor," Santiago said, nodding toward a skinny girl in a tight dress and high heels smiling at me across the crowed night club. "Go ask her to dance."

Santiago had brought me to Havana's version of a discotheque and I was grateful to my boss for trying to fix me up. But the scene just wasn't working for me.

For one thing, I wasn't used to the music.

Don't get me wrong. I loved the rumba tunes the deejay was spinning. It's in my blood. But my groove for dancing was Motown. I could shake a leg with pop rock, too. Before the whole flower child thing got rolling, I'd picked up chicks at teen dance clubs in Hialeah and North Miami.

The people dancing here, though, were like Arthur Murray students doing graduate work on cha-cha twirls and mambo footwork.

"I don't know how to dance like this," I told Santiago.

"I'll lay a stone in the creek for you, my yanqui friend," my boss said, then walked to the guy spinning records and whispered in his ear.

Santiago was the best boss I'd ever had. The guy was funny and cool. He didn't give orders. He'd say things like, "Nestor, there are better ways to meet a pretty nurse than taking a visitor who slipped on those wet leaves to the hospital."

Tall, lean and the color of ebony, Santiago walked with

an easy stride, always smiling. And females noticed.

I was familiar with those looks from the ladies. In the States, my hair and flair made an impression.

But here? I had nothing special going for me.

Looks weren't the only thing holding me back. I spoke Spanish perfectly – or as perfectly as any Cuban speaks it, anyway. The problem was, when it came to conversations... I was just plain dull.

Young Cubans had their own slang. Unfamiliar with the lingo, I became the clueless foreign exchange student back in the States who everyone smiled at but never got invited to parties.

The hip jive I'd soaked up back in Miami made no sense to anyone here – even if they'd understood English. My conversations were dry. And that's a turnoff for women everywhere. My mojo was gone, man.

If all that wasn't bad enough, I had another strike against me. I could not stop thinking about Elise. Who else would ever measure up?

Then something happened that brought the whole disco to a standstill.

Instead of another conga tune, the first bars of *Mustang Sally* started coming from the speakers.

As the dancefloor thinned to a half dozen couples, Santiago walked up to me. "The deejay had to dig deep in his collection for this one," he said, gently pushing me toward the skinny girl. "This is your chance."

I'd asked girls to dance before, hundreds of times. But I'd never been shaking like this. Mustering my courage, I held out my palm to the skinny girl. She smiled, nodded, and followed me to the dance floor.

Getting down with the beat, I started with a smooth

Shing-a-Ling.

As Wilson Pickett hit the bridge, I closed my eyes and broke into the Philly Dog. Aw, hell yeah. Cruiser was groovin' now, y'all.

There were a few snickers at first. Then, the whole night club erupted into laughter. All the others on the floor stopped dancing. Every eye in the place was fixed on my dance partner and me.

The skinny girl gave me a pity smile, then slouched off the dancefloor.

My face was a chili pepper by the time I got back to Santiago.

He smiled gently, patted me on the shoulder and said, "Nestor, you still speak Spanish like a native, but you dance with an American accent."

# 63

**I'D JUST** gotten off the bus still wearing my zoo khakis when a guy on the sidewalk in a starched *guayabera* and two-toned wing tips opened his arms wide. "Primo! I'd know you anywhere," he said with a smile, then gave me a hug.

After a moment, I said, "Emilio?" About twenty when I'd left Cuba, my step-cousin had not changed all that much. A gaudy gold ID bracelet engraved with his name in curly letters would have tipped me off anyway. The matching gold necklace outside his shirt told me Emilio had some coin – and wanted you to know it.

"I'm happy to see you didn't forget me! Let's have a *cafecito*, primo. We need to get acquainted again," he said, nodding toward the counter of a bodega with an expresso machine.

When the storekeeper saw my step-cousin, the guy gave Emilio a greasy smile. "How are you today, Emilio? What can I get for you?"

Emilio held up two fingers and winked.

The storekeeper served us two *tacitas* of thick, steaming black coffee with a small glass of cold water on the side.

After a sip of brew, Emilio said, "At least we still have good coffee, eh?"

"For sure," I said.

"How do you like being back?"

"It's a big change," I said, not wanting to lie.

Emilio drained his *tacita*, gulped down the glass of

water, and slapped some coins on the counter. "Finish your coffee. Let's go someplace where we can talk, primo," he said putting his arm around my shoulder.

We walked to a small park with a dry fountain and grass sparse enough to pass for green psoriasis. Emilio sat on a bench and waved for me to sit next to him. "I could use your help with something important, primo," he said.

"I'll do whatever I can," I said, sitting down.

"I heard you were a hippie back in La Yuma, is that right?"

I nodded. "Yeah, you could say that."

"Are any of your hippie friends back in Miami friendly with the perico?"

My eyebrows rose. I was surprised Emilio knew the street code for coke.

"Why do you want to know?" I asked.

"You lived in La Yuma. You understand how business works. We have a big opportunity here, primo. There's a huge potential market for perico in La Habana. Anyone with access to a steady supply could do quite well here."

I saw where this was going. "You want me to connect you with someone in Miami who can supply you with cocaine."

Emilio smiled and slapped my knee. "You're smart, muchacho. I knew getting in touch with you would be a good idea. You know the right kind of people, speak perfect English and can blend right in. I couldn't do this alone."

After all I'd been through, there was no fucking way I was going to get involved in drug smuggling. Still, Emilio was family – sort of. So I tried a dodge. "Does your father know about this?"

"My father is behind the times, primo. That's why he's still poor. His idea for the future of Cuba is to keep spreading the poverty around. I'm a patriot. I want to bring back wealth to this country. People with money in their pockets create jobs."

"And you plan to be one of those with the money in your pocket."

"Why not? Somebody has to show the *cojones* to make things better."

I rose to my feet." I can't help you with this, Emilio. I'm sorry."

His features hardened as he stood to face me. "Can't help me or won't help me?"

"It doesn't make any difference. My answer is still no."

Emilio gave me a hard stare for a moment, then said. "I thought you were smart, Nestor. What you're doing is not."

I shrugged, trying to stay calm. "See you around, Emilio," I said and walked away.

# 64

**THE NEXT** day, after stepping off the bus, I saw Emilio again. Wearing a skin-tight banlon with stripes the colors of a toucan beak, my step-cousin was leaning against a building as a stream of workers and students walked by.

He waved me over. This was starting to get old.

I hadn't said anything to Tio Lalo about running into Emilio. There was no point. Tio was ashamed of his son, with good reason. I didn't want to make Tio feel worse.

"Follow me, primo. We need to talk," he said, walking into the narrow space between two buildings. About a dozen steps in, the corridor widened into an alcove. Three guys were waiting there.

The biggest one grabbed me by the collar and shoved me against the wall. The other two pinned my arms.

Walking in front of me, Emilio put his face close to mine. "Do you think you're something special here, Nestor?" he asked. His breath smelled like cigarettes and coffee.

I shook my head. "I never said that."

"No? You turned and walked away from your older cousin. That's a sign of disrespect," Emilio said, then glanced toward the big guy. "Isn't that right, Lazaro?"

"Very disrespectful," Lazaro agreed.

Emilio turned his eyes back to me. "I'm willing to overlook this insult, primo. You've been away and you've forgotten our ways. But I want you to reconsider my request," he said. "Look, I've got uniforms behind me, Nestor. They'll protect everyone connected with me. You won't be in any danger. But there's another side to that coin. Do you understand?"

"I understand," I said, nodding my head. This was not a time to be brave. "I'll do what you asked."

Emilio smiled and nodded to his goons. They let me go.

"You go home now and enjoy your dinner with my father and his wife," my step-cousin said. "I'll be in touch about our little trip."

# 65

**OUR GAME** of dominoes after dinner at Tio and Tia's had become an evening ritual.

I wasn't very good. But I loved watching them turn taunting into an art form. Normally kind and gentle, once the dominoes were shuffled, my aunt and uncle became ruthless.

With two pieces left, Tio was scoping the board like a vulture circling a roadkill.

Tia cleared her throat loudly and began drumming her fingers on the table. When Tio finally made his play, she said, "My mother's cow could bring a calf to term in the time it takes you to play, Lalo."

"Finding a bull interested in her ugly cow would take even longer, old woman."

"Old woman, eh? That's pretty funny coming from somebody who taught Methuselah how to tie his shoelaces," she said, then slapped her last piece on the table and yelled, "Domino!"

With the game over and Tio putting away the pieces, the opportunity I'd been waiting for arrived.

"I ran into Emilio the other day," I said, handing Tio the lid to the domino box. "He seems to be doing well."

Tio waited until my aunt was out of the room, then quietly said, "Stay away from Emilio."

"Why, Tio?" I hated to mislead my uncle, but I wanted to check out Emilio's story about having the authorities in his pocket.

"The things he does are against the law."

"Then why isn't he in jail?"

"Emilio has low friends in high places, Nestor."

I gulped. "All the way to the beard?"

"Not that high," Tio whispered, shaking his head. "But his friends are still very powerful." Then in a normal voice he said, "Let's go listen to the boxing match. Teofilo is fighting tonight."

While Tio and Tia sat by the radio, mesmerized by the fight, all I could think about was Emilio. He had *me* on the ropes, without a doubt. If I defied him, Emilio might get me deported, put in jail – or worse.

# 66

**A WEEK** later, I was about a block from home when Emilio's burly thug, Lazaro, stopped me on the street.

"Be at the park with the fountain tonight," he said with a stone-hard stare. "Bring a bag with clothes for four days."

So this was it. Emilio was calling in his marker. With no other choice, I asked, "What time?"

"After dark," Lazaro said, then walked away.

Around midnight, a '59 Impala pulled to the curb near my park bench. "Get in," Emilio called out from behind the wheel.

I slid inside, Pancho in hand. The two-way radio I saw under the Impala's dash confirmed Emilio was no ordinary hoodlum.

"I'm sure my father and his wife noticed you were leaving with a bag," Emilio said. "What did you tell them?"

"I said some of the zoo workers had been asked to volunteer planting sugar cane."

"You have a gift for lying, Nestor," he said, smiling. I'll need to watch you closely."

Neither of us said anything more as Emilio drove out of the city, heading west. That made one thing clear. Emilio's boat wasn't docked in Havana's harbor.

After crossing the Rio Almendares, my step-cousin broke the silence.

"When we get to Miami, I want you to connect me only with yanqui suppliers. No Latin Americans – and especially, no Cubans.”

“Emilio, every dealer in Miami buys their coke from Peru. Why not go to the Peruvians directly?”

“That’s none of your business. Just do what you’re told.”

I shrugged. There must have been some bad blood between Cuba and Peru that I didn’t know about.

“Where are we going to dock when we get to Miami?” I asked. “There’s a Coast Guard station at the mouth of the harbor. I doubt your boat has a U.S. registry.”

“The helmsman will drop us off in the mangroves near Big Pine Key. They have a bus station there. That’s how we’ll get to Miami. He’ll pick us up four days later at the same spot.”

I rubbed my temples. Oh, no. Not the bus again. All I could see in my future was misery.

Turning off the main road, Emilio drove along a narrow path through scrubby bushes until we reached the coast. He stopped the car, turned off the lights, and said, “This is it.”

Stepping out into the darkness with Pancho on my shoulder, I could make out a dock and a speedboat as the ocean glimmered in the moonlight. I recognized the hulking shape of Lazaro walking toward us from the dock.

“The helmsman isn’t here yet,” Lazaro told Emilio.

“*Coño!* Nothing on this island happens on time,” Emilio said. “Take this one to the dock and keep an eye on him,” he told Lazaro, nodding toward me. “I’m going to check with the twins.”

I could hear Emilio firing up the two-way radio in the car as we walked away. The sound faded as we reached the dock. Emilio didn’t want me to hear his conversation.

At the end of the dock, Lazaro lit a cigarette, looking

out toward the ocean.

I glanced back toward the car. Emilio was still inside.

I've never had big balls like Peanut. If there was an easy way out of trouble, I took it. But the time had come for some *cojones*. This boat was fueled and ready. It would get me to the States. What would I do after getting there? I had no idea. But anything seemed better than becoming Emilio's bitch.

When Lazaro took another drag, I shoved him into the water.

Then I released the boat's line to the dock, threw Pancho aboard and jumped inside.

Getting behind the helm, I reached for the starter key. Shit. It wasn't there.

I checked the pocket next to the helm. No luck.

I looked behind me. Emilio was running toward the dock and Lazaro was scrambling to climb aboard the boat's stern.

Ducking into the cabin, I looked around, my hands shaking.

Then I saw it. On a string hanging from a peg on the wall was the ignition key.

Back at the helm, I put in the key and turned the ignition. The engine sputtered and died. I looked back and saw a puff of smoke rise behind the stern.

"C'mon, baby. Start," I pleaded, turning the key again.

With a throaty growl, the inboard V8 roared into life.

I pushed the throttle full ahead. When the boat lurched away from the dock, the rush I felt was like an orgasm. Emilio wouldn't reach the boat in time.

Then I remembered Lazaro.

Turning around I saw his upper body inside the boat,

struggling to hold on against the pull of the wake. Looking around, I spotted a boat hook clamped along the gunnel.

With the throttle locked on full, I pointed the boat toward the open sea and ran toward Lazaro.

I reached the stern and raised the boat hook above my head. Lazaro looked up at me, eyes wide with terror. "Let go!" I screamed.

Lazaro slid back into the water, arms flailing as he went.

Hoping Lazaro had survived, I ran back to the helm and steered away from the coast.

I was sure Emilio would use the radio to send another boat after me.

I needed to be somewhere else – fast.

# 67

**THE WAVES** slapping against the hull made a steady whap-whap-whap over the drone of the engine. Keeping the ball to the wall on the throttle, I steered toward a reflection on the horizon from a melon slice moon.

I looked back toward the lights of the coast fading into the distance. The thumping of my heart changed tempo from a Tito Puente conga to a ballad by Desi Arnaz.

No boat leaving shore was going to catch me now. But if Emilio's friends in uniform included the Cuban Coast Guard, he could radio my heading to a ship on patrol off-shore that might cut me off.

There was nothing I could do about that. My only hope was to keep running hard and reach U.S. waters before they caught me.

I'm not a whiz at geography. And I'm sure as hell not a navigator.

But I knew getting a boat from Havana to Florida was like trying to figure out which direction will get you down from a mountain. Just head downhill.

In this case, downhill was north.

Heading north, I'd hit land somewhere in the Keys or up the Florida coast. That destination was precise enough for me. All I needed was enough moonlight to keep the needle on the boat's compass pointing toward the N for four or five hours.

Fuel was not a problem. The tanks were topped up for

a trip to the Keys and back. I only needed enough juice to go one way.

I wasn't safe by a long shot, though. If the engine conked out, I'd be caught by the Cubans or die of exposure and wind up as shark meat.

But as more time behind the helm passed, my mind wandered to a place I hadn't expected... my father.

Without my old man, I wouldn't have been able to swipe this boat.

Most elementary school kids had a mom at home during summer vacations. Me, I went to work with my dad at the boatyard all summer. I loved it, too. The odd jobs and rough banter among the guys were a blast. And I learned a lot about boats during those summers.

But in junior high, I discovered books. Instead of working around the boatyard, I'd hole up in a cabin cruiser with another Heinlein or Bradbury. This pissed off my dad. He thought my teachers were filling my head with fantasies about a life I could never have. Colleges and office jobs were for rich kids, he told me more than once.

By the time I got to high school, I was stocking groceries during the summer. Not long after graduation, I moved out on my own.

Looking back on it now, it probably hurt my dad that Peanut took a job in the boatyards but not his own son.

Seeing Tia Clara's pictures of my mom had opened my eyes to the pain my father had endured alone, without complaint.

If I made it back to Miami, I'd thank my father for bringing me to the States and the sacrifices he'd made.

But right now, making it back to Miami was still a very big if.

# 68

**I'D BEEN** cruising for about three hours and hadn't seen any other boats. The engine was still running steady. Maybe, just maybe, I might make it to Florida.

But that really wasn't the end of my problems. I was a fugitive there too.

In reality, I had just traded one clusterfuck for another. Like I said, I hadn't really thought this whole thing through when I pulled the snatch-and-run with this boat.

By now, there were probably bench warrants for Nestor Cruz in every police department on the Eastern Seaboard. Once I landed in Florida, I'd be on the run again, looking over my shoulder every minute.

If the U.S. Coast Guard found me at sea, a background check would send me straight to jail. Do not pass GO. Do not collect $200 for lawyer fees.

Then it hit me.

Who could prove I was Nestor Cruz? I was going to land with no I.D. on a boat from Cuba. For all they knew, I could be just another desperate Cuban refugee who made his way to Florida.

The first thing I'd need to do is create a new identity. What was my name? Who were my parents? Where was I born?

There were a thousand details to work out. Screw up on any one of them, and my ass would land in jail. I had a lot to do – and I didn't have much time.

Making sure the compass pointed north, I stuck the boat hook through the ship's wheel, locking it in place. Then I ducked into the cabin.

The first thing I saw was Pancho. "I love you, buddy. But it's time for you to go," I said. A refugee arriving by boat with a PanAm flight bag might raise red flags.

I was about to unzip Pancho for anything I'd want to keep when I saw something else, deeper in the cabin.

Another travel bag.

Apparently, Emilio had already stowed his gear.

A small bubble of thought started rising in my brain. My excitement began jacking up as a realization grew.

I rushed to the bag and unzipped it.

Inside were fat stacks of U.S. dollars, each neatly sealed in plastic.

# 69

**"HOLY FUCKING** shit!" I screamed and broke into a rumba, dancing around the cabin – until I hit my head on the ceiling.

The pain brought me back down to earth.

Unless I was very careful, that money would be nothing more than evidence against me. Refugees didn't wash ashore with bags of cash

Back at the helm, I spotted my first island.

About a quarter mile ahead, the island was a dull patch of darkness, not much bigger than a house, in the glimmering black water. I cut the motor to quarter speed.

Cruising slowly past the island, I finally saw my destination on the horizon.

Like a string of Christmas tree lights lying flat across the water was the Overseas Highway.

I had no idea where I was along that long stretch of US 1 that hopscotched the islands between the coast of Florida and Key West. It didn't matter. Any part of it was U.S. soil.

Once I reached it, I was safe. Thanks to LBJ, any Cuban seeking asylum in the U.S. would be eligible to apply for a green card. No other nation had this privilege.

But I still needed to be careful. If I ran aground on a sandbar and was spotted by the U.S. Coast Guard, I'd be returned to Cuba within sight of my salvation.

Slowly guiding the boat between these little islands was

agony. Twice I had to double back. The distance between the islands ahead looked too tight. I couldn't risk going between them.

Then the worst of my fears came true.

My chest hit the helm as the boat struck a sand bar.

"Shit!" I said, pulling the throttle into reverse.

No luck. I was stuck.

I wasn't enough of a seaman to know if the tide was rising or falling. In any case, it was crazy to wait out here. I'd be easy to spot by a Coast Guard patrol once the sun rose.

I needed to get this boat off the sandbar – now.

Turning off the engine, I walked to the bow and looked down into the inky water, my chest starting to pound.

I was scared shitless of sharks. I never went much past my knees at the beach. It wasn't because I couldn't swim. I was Johnny Weissmuller in a pool. But swim in the ocean? No fucking way.

Except that now, I had to get into that creepy black sea or spend the rest of my life with a prison number on my shirt.

Hands trembling, I lowered myself into the water. My feet touched bottom with the water above my knees. I looked around, expecting to see a fin breaking the surface. Sharks could attack in very shallow water.

Without my weight, the boat rose slightly. Digging my feet into the sand, I put my shoulder against the bow and pushed.

The boat didn't budge.

In a panic, I tried rocking the boat, desperately pushing up and down on the gunnel like a dog humping a leg. When the boat finally broke loose, a rush of joy surged through me – followed by a wave of terror.

The boat was drifting away from me and nearly out of reach.

I lunged and got one hand on a line cleat. I got my other hand on the gunnel as my legs thrashed wildly in the suddenly deeper water.

Hanging by my fingertips, I inched along the gunnel toward the stern where the waterline was low enough to climb inside, the whole time sure a shark was about to tear off one of my legs.

Back in the boat, I was relieved – for about a minute. Then a sense of doom set in. At this rate, it might be daylight before I got to the Overseas Highway.

As I stared toward the distant string of lights, my father's voice rose in my head. "*Buscale la vuelta,*" the old man said. In English, his words meant "find a way around the problem."

I slapped my forehead. Instead of steering toward the highway through the islands, maybe I should try to find a way around them.

Gunning the engine to full throttle, I swung the boat to the right. I'd run parallel to the Overseas Highway until I saw clear water between us.

Within ten minutes, I'd found a safe passage.

I beached the boat on the sands of a deserted stretch along the highway. There, between a pair of palms, I buried the bag with Emilio's cash.

Then I took the boat back out into the ocean. A couple of hundred yards from shore, I cut the engine. This would be the hardest part.

I needed to sink this boat. Bringing it ashore was too risky. The boat might be traced back to Emilio – and then to me.

After I opened all the seacocks, the boat began to sink. Now came the part I'd been dreading – getting into a black sea I was sure was teeming with sharks.

The boat was almost completely underwater when I took off my shoes and started swimming toward shore. I tensed up with every stroke, expecting the chomp of razor-sharp teeth on my flesh.

To distract me from the fear and keep my swimming at a steady pace, I recited *Georgie Porgie* in my head.

*Georgie Porgie* (stroke) *pudding'n pie* (stroke) *Kiss'd the girls* (stroke) *and made them cry* (stroke) *Georgie Porgie* (stroke) *pudding'n pie...*

When my feet finally touched sand, I sprinted out of that water like Bullet Bob Hayes going for the gold.

Walking carefully in my bare feet, I made my way to US 1. The mile marker there read 47.

With a hint of dawn glowing in the east, I started walking north along the empty two-lane road.

Watching where I stepped, I passed marinas, gift stores, bait shops and restaurants – all of them dark and closed. With my feet getting raw, I came to a chain link fence topped with barbed wire. A sign near the gate read:

U.S. COAST GUARD STATION MARATHON.

## 70

**"WOULD YOU** like some more coffee, Jose?" the ensign asked, putting a hand on my shoulder.

I held up my palm. "No, zank ju. Ju are bery kind." Like every Cuban kid who'd grown up in Miami, I had my father's thick accent down cold.

The young officer walked away, leaving me in the empty mess hall. The skeleton crew on night watch at the Coast Guard station had stashed me here for now. At nine, they'd find someone who could drive me to the INS office in Miami. In the meantime, they'd given me dry clothes, some slippers, and a coffee from the vending machine.

I'd kept my story simple when I'd walked into the Coast Guard station an hour earlier with my clothes still wet.

My name was Jose Paz I'd said, using my father's accent. The boat I'd stolen in Cuba had sunk just off the Florida coast and I'd barely made it to shore.

I made Jose's history easy for me to remember. I used the same neighborhood in Havana where I'd lived and the same schools I attended. My parents were conveniently buried and I had no other close relatives in Havana or the States. I'd studied English at the "junibearcity."

I felt pretty sure the story would hold up. With no diplomatic relations between the U.S. and Cuba, how could they really check out anything I said?

Recalling Emilio's plan for this night, a thought came up that made me smile. Thank God I wasn't getting on a goddam bus again.

The mess hall door opened. "Come with me, Jose," the ensign called out, crooking his finger. "We'll take you to Miami now."

Walking down the hall, I began to think ahead.

Once I was settled, I'd make my way back to mile marker 47. From there, Jose Paz would have the means to do things Nestor Cruz never could.

In time, I'd find a safe way to see my father again. I might even make my way back to Canada. When I could, I'd write to Tio and Tia to let them know I was safe.

Not many people got a chance to wipe the slate clean.

I wasn't going to waste it.

# HAPPY TRAILS

I turned seventy this year. I may live a while longer. But most of the sand in my hourglass is already on the bottom. I'm okay with that. In any case, I don't have much choice, do I?

I'd like to tell you I did amazing things with my life. That would make a great ending. But in a way, something better happened. My daughter did that for me.

Eva graduated from Stanford and fell in with some tech geeks in Palo Alto. Their startup's IPO made her a millionaire overnight. Not bad for a kid raised in a Midwest college town by a professor and a freshman-year dropout. Elise always insisted Eva's brains came from her side of the family. Until the day he passed, my father agreed.

I wondered about Tia and Tio for a long time. When the cold war thawed in the early 2000s, I got in touch with them on a weepy call over a sketchy phone line. They were thrilled to know I was safe. Emilio was not as lucky.

He and his "low friends in high places" were arrested and executed by a Cuban firing squad for drug trafficking in 1989.

Not that it matters much these days, but the suspicion of murder by Nestor Suarez and Maxwell O'Connor slipped into the ether in the late 80s when the FBI finally cracked the Dixie Mafia. The government's chief snitch fingered a number of hired killers who'd gunned-down small-time dealers on the Dixie Mafia's turf. Among them was Erna "Fish" Herring who had taken out Vardon and the Viceroys.

I get a card from Peanut every Christmas and a phone call now and then. He and Cookie raised a slew of kids on their farm in Manitoba. Now, they're empty nesters who like to play golf and take European riverboat cruises.

You might think that coming to the States from Cuba as a kid would be the most significant event of my life. But looking back, I divide my years into two parts: before and after the day I took the keys for that Mustang to Paducah.

That trip revealed a lot of things, about me and the people in my life. I won't bore you with an old man's homilies. There are more than enough books around on that kind of shit.

But I will say this: The man who came back from that crazy-ass adventure was a far better person than the one who left.

Peace and love to you always,
Cruiser

## OTHER BOOKS BY RAUL RAMOS Y SANCHEZ

AMERICA LIBRE (Class H Trilogy - Book 1)
HOUSE DIVIDED (Class H Trilogy - Book 2)
PANCHO LAND (Class H Trilogy - Book 3)
THE SKINNY YEARS
KING ROBIN (written as R. A. Moss)


## REVIEWS FOR PREVIEWS BOOKS

**"HIGHLY ORIGINAL"**
Library Journal

**"PROVOCATIVE"**
USA Today

**"SWEEPING, INTENSE"**
Publishers Weekly

**"THRILLING AND VIBRANT"**
Author James Rollins

## ABOUT THE AUTHOR

Cuban-born Raul Ramos y Sanchez grew up in Miami's cultural kaleidoscope before becoming a long-time resident of the U.S. Midwest. After a successful career in advertising that included founding an ad agency with offices in Ohio and California, Ramos turned to more personally significant work.

His previous novels include the Class H Trilogy (*America Libre, House Divided* and *Pancho Land*), *The Skinny Years* and *King Robin* written as R. A. Moss

The author and his work have been featured on television, radio and print publications across the country along with a host of online media sources.

Visit Raul's website at:
**RAULRAMOS.COM**